Haste and Waste

Oliver Optic

Contents

HASTE AND WASTE

BY

Oliver Optic

BIOGRAPHY AND BIBLIOGRAPHY

William Taylor Adams, American author, better known and loved by boys and girls through his pseudonym "Oliver Optic," was born July 30, 1822, in the town of Medway, Norfolk County, Massachusetts, about twenty-five miles from Boston. For twenty years he was a teacher in the Public Schools of Boston, where he came in close contact with boy life. These twenty years taught him how to reach the boy's heart and interest as the popularity of his books attest.

His story writing began in 1850 when he was twenty-eight years old and his first book was published in 1853. He also edited "The Oliver Optic Magazine," "The Student and Schoolmate," "Our Little Ones."

Mr. Adams died at the age of seventy-five years, in Boston, March 27, 1897.

He was a prolific writer and his stories are most attractive and unobjectionable. Most of his books were published in series. Probably the most famous of these is "The Boat Club Series" which comprises the following titles:

"The Boat Club," "All Aboard," "Now or Never," "Try Again," "Poor and Proud," "Little by Little." All of these titles will be found in this edition.

Other well-known series are his "Soldier Boy Series," "Sailor Boy Series," "Woodville Stories." The "Woodville Stories" will also be found in this edition.

CHAPTER I
THE SQUALL ON THE LAKE

Stand by, Captain John!" shouted Lawry Wilford, a stout boy of fourteen, as he stood at the helm of a sloop, which was going before the wind up Lake Champlain.

"What's the matter, Lawry?" demanded the captain.

"We're going to have a squall," continued the young pilot, as he glanced at the tall peaks of the Adirondacks.

There was a squall in those clouds, in the judgment of Lawry Wilford; but having duly notified the captain of the impending danger to his craft, he did not assume any further responsibility in the management of the sloop. It was very quiet on the lake; the water was smooth, and the tiny waves sparkled in the bright sunshine. There was no roll of distant thunder to admonish the voyagers, and the youth at the helm was so much accustomed to squalls and tempests, which are of frequent occurrence on the lake, that they had no terrors to him. It was dinner-time, and the young pilot, fearful that the unexpected guest might reduce the rations to a low ebb for the second table, was more concerned about this matter than about the squall.

Captain John, as he was familiarly called on board the *Missisque,* which was the name of the sloop, was not a man to be cheated out of any portion of his dinner by the approach of a squall; and though his jaws may have moved more rapidly after the announcement of the young pilot, he did not neglect even the green-apple pies, the first of the season, prepared with care and skill by Mrs. Captain John, who resided on board, and did "doctor's" duty at the galley. Captain John did not abate a single mouthful of the meal, though he knew how rapidly the mountain showers and squalls travel over the lake. The sloop did not usually make more than four or five miles an hour, being deeply laden with lumber, which was piled up so high on the deck that the mainsail had to be reefed, to make room for it.

The passenger, Mr. Randall, was a director of a country bank, journeying to Shoreham, about twenty miles above the point where he had embarked in the *Missisque*. He had crossed the lake in the ferry, intending to take the steamer at Westport for his destination. Being a man who was always in a hurry, but never in season, he had reached the steamboat landing just in time to see the boat moving off. Procuring a wherry, and a boy to row it, he had boarded the *Missisque* as she passed up the lake; and, though the sloop was not a passenger-boat, Captain John had consented to land him at Shoreham.

Mr. Randall was a landsman, and had a proper respect for squalls and tempests, even on a fresh-water lake. He heard the announcement of Lawry Wilford with a feeling of dread and apprehension, and straightway began to conjure up visions of a terrible shipwreck, and of sole survivors, clinging with the madness of desperation to broken spars, in the midst of the storm-tossed waters. But Mr. Randall was a director of a country bank, and a certain amount of dignity was expected and required of him. His official position before the people of Vermont demanded that he should not give way to idle fears. If Captain Jones, who was not a bank director, could keep cool, it was Mr. Randall's solemn duty to remain unmoved, or at least to appear to remain so.

The passenger finished the first course of the dinner, which Mrs. Captain John had made a little more elaborate than usual, in honor of the distinguished guest; but he complained of the smallness of his appetite, and it was evident that he did not enjoy the meal after the brief colloquy between the skipper and the pilot. He was nervous; his dignity was a "bore" to him, and was maintained at an immense sacrifice of personal ease; but he persevered until a piece of the dainty green-apple pie was placed before him, when he lacerated the tender feelings of Mrs. Captain John by abruptly leaving the table and rushing on deck.

This hurried movement was hardly to be regarded as a sacrifice of his dignity, for it was made with what even the skipper's lady was compelled to allow was a reasonable excuse.

"Gracious!" exclaimed Mr. Randall, as the tempting piece of green-apple pie, reeking with indigenous juices was placed before him.

At the same moment the bank director further indicated his astonishment and horror by slapping both hands upon his breast in a style worthy of Brutus when Rome was in peril.

"What's the matter, squire?" demanded Captain John, dropping his knife and fork, and suspending the operation of his vigorous jaws till an explanation could be obtained.

"I've left my coat on deck," replied Mr. Randall, rising from his chair.

"It's just as safe there as 'twould be on your back, squire," added the skipper.

"There's six thousand dollars in the pocket of that coat," said the bank director, with a gasp of apprehension. "Where's my coat?" demanded he.

"There it is," replied Lawry Wilford, pointing to the garment under the rail. "We had a flaw of wind just now, and it came pretty near being blowed overboard."

"Gracious!" exclaimed Mr. Randall, as he clutched the coat. "I'm too careless to live! There's six thousand dollars in a pocket of that coat."

"Six thousand dollars!" ejaculated Lawry, whose ideas of such a sum of money were very indefinite. "I should say you ought not to let it lie round loose in this way."

"I'm very careless; but the money is safe," continued the director.

"Stand by, Captain John!" suddenly shouted Lawry, with tremendous energy, as he put the helm down. The squall was coming up the lake in the track of the *Missisque*; a dull, roaring sound was heard astern; and all the mountain peaks had disappeared, closed in by the dense volume of black clouds. The episode of the bank director's coat had distracted the attention of the young pilot for a moment, and he had not observed the rapid swoop of the squall, as it bore down upon the sloop. He leaped over the piles of lumber to the forecastle, and had cast loose the peak-halyard, when Captain John tumbled up the companionway in time to see that he had lingered too long over the green-apple pie, and that one piece would have been better for his vessel, if not for him.

"Let go the throat-halyard!" roared he. "Down with the mainsail! down with the mainsail!"

Lawry did not need any prompting to do his duty; but before he could let go the throat-halyard, the squall was upon the sloop. Mr. Randall had seized hold of the rail, and was crouching beneath the bulwark, expecting to go to the bottom of the lake, for he was too much excited to make a comparison of the specific gravities of pine boards and fresh water, and therefore did not realize that lumber would float, and not sink.

The squall did its work in an instant; and before the bank director had fairly begun to tremble, the rotten mainsail of the *Missisque* was blown into ribbons, and the "flapping flitters" were streaming in the air. Piece after piece was detached from the bolt-rope, and disappeared in the heavy atmosphere. The sloop, in obedience to her helm, came about, and was now headed down the lake. The rain began to fall in torrents, and Mr. Randall was as uncomfortable as the director of a country bank could be.

"Go below, sir!" shouted Captain John to the unhappy man.

"Is it safe?" asked Mr. Randall.

"Safe enough."

"Won't she sink?"

"Sink? no; she can't sink," replied the skipper. "The wu'st on't's over now."

The fury of the squall was spent in a moment, and then the fury of Captain John began to gather, as he saw the remnants of the sail flapping at the gaff and the boom. The *Missisque* and her cargo were safe, and not a single one of the precious lives of her crew had been sacrificed; but the skipper was as dissatisfied as the skipper of a lake sloop could be; more so, probably, than if the vessel had gone to the bottom, and left him clinging for life to a lone spar on the angry waters, for men are often more reasonable under great than under small misfortunes.

"Why didn't you let go that throat-halyard?" said he, as he walked forward to where the young pilot stood.

"I did," replied Lawry quietly.

"You did! What was the use of lettin' it go after the squall had split the sail? Why didn't you do it sooner?"

"I did it as soon as I saw the squall coming down on us."

"Why didn't you see it before then?" growled Captain John.

"I told you the squall was coming half an hour ago. Why didn't you come on deck, and attend to your vessel?"

"Don't be sassy," said Captain John.

"I'm not the skipper of this craft. If I had been, that sail would have been safe.

I told you the squall was coming, and after that I did the best I could."

"You ain't good for nothin' 'board a vessel. I thought you knew enough to take in sail when you saw a squall comin'."

"I should have taken in sail long ago if I had thought the captain didn't know enough to come on deck when there was a squall coming up," replied Lawry.

"I don't want nothin' more of you."

"And I don't want anything more of you," added Lawry smartly. "I've got almost home."

"What do you s'pose I'm goin' to do here, eighty mile from Whitehall, with the mainsail blowed clean out?" snarled Captain John, as he followed Lawry.

"Mind your vessel better than you have, I hope."

"Don't be sassy, boy."

"You needn't growl at me because you neglected your duty. I did mine. I was casting off the halyards when the squall came."

"Why didn't you do it before? That's what I want to know."

"I had no orders from the captain. Men on board a vessel don't take in sail till they are told to do so. When I saw the squall coming, half an hour ago, I let you know it; that was all I had to do with it."

"I don't want you in this vessel; you are too smart for me," continued Captain John.

"I'll leave her just as soon as we get to Port Rock," said Lawry, sitting down on the rail.

The rain ceased in a few moments, and the skipper ordered the jib, which had before been useless, to be set. At the invitation of Mrs. Captain John, Lawry went below and ate his dinner, to which he felt himself entitled, for he was working his passage up from Plattsburg. By the time he had disposed of the last piece of green-apple pie on board, the *Missisque* was before Port Rock, which was the home of the young pilot, and he saw his father's ferry-boat at the shore as he came on deck.

"Will you put me ashore here, Captain John?" asked Lawry.

"Yes, I will; and I'm glad to get rid of you," replied the captain testily.

"I think I will land here, also," added the bank director. "Now you have lost your sail, I'm afraid you won't get along very fast."

"I don't expect I shall. I sha'n't get to Shoreham till to-morrow morning with this wind. I'm sorry it happened so; but that boy didn't mind what he was about."

"The captain didn't mind what he was about," added Lawry. "He needn't lay it to me, when it was all his own fault."

"I will cross the lake, and get a horse at Pointville, so that I shall be in Shoreham by five o'clock," continued the bank director.

Captain John ordered one of the men to pull Mr. Randall and Lawry ashore in the boat, and in a few minutes they were landed at Port Rock.

CHAPTER II
THE PORT ROCK FERRY

Lawrence Wilford was a full-fledged water-fowl. From his earliest childhood he had paddled in Lake Champlain. His father had a small place, consisting of ten acres of land with a small cottage; but it was still encumbered with a mortgage, as it had been for twenty years, though the note had passed through several hands, and had been three times renewed. John Wilford was not a very sagacious nor a very energetic man, and had not distinguished himself in the race for wealth or for fame. He wanted to be rich, but he was not willing to pay the price of riches.

His place was a short distance from the village of Port Rock, and John Wilford, at the time he had purchased the land and built his house, had established a ferry, which had been, and was still, his principal means of support; for there was considerable travel between Port Rock and Pointville, on the Vermont side of the lake.

The ferryman was a poor man, and was likely to remain a poor man to the end of his life. Hardly a day passed in which he did not sigh to be rich, and complain of the unequal and unjust distribution of property. He could point to a score of men who had not worked half so hard as he had, in his own opinion, that had made fortunes, or at least won a competence, while he was as poor as ever, and in danger of having his place taken away from him. People said that John Wilford was lazy; that he did not make the most of his land, and that his ferry, with closer attention to the wants of passengers, might be made to pay double the amount he made from it. He permitted the weeds to grow in his garden, and compelled people to wait by the hour for a passage across the lake.

John Wilford wondered that he could not grow rich, that he could not pay off the mortgage on his place. He seldom sat down to dinner without grumbling at his hard lot. His wife was a sensible woman. She did not wonder that he did not grow rich; only that he contrived to keep out of the poorhouse. She was the mother of eight children, and if he had been half as smart as she was, prosperity would have smiled upon the family. As it was, her life was filled up with struggles to make the ends meet; but, though she had the worst of it, she did not complain, and did all she could to comfort and encourage her thriftless husband.

The oldest son was as near like his father as one person could be like another. He was eighteen years old, and was an idle and dissolute fellow. Lawrence, the second son, inherited his mother's tack and energy. He was observing and enterprising, and had already made a good reputation as a boatman and pilot. He had worked in various capacities on board of steamers, canal-boats, sloops, and schooners, and in five years had visited every part of the lake from Whitehall to St. Johns.

Speaking technically, his bump of locality was large, and he was as familiar with the navigation of the lake as any pilot on its waters. Indeed, he had occasionally served as a pilot on board steamers and other vessels, which had earned for him the name of the Young Pilot, by which he was often called. But his business was not piloting, for there was but little of this work to be done. Unlike his father, he was willing to do anything which would afford him a fair compensation, and in his five years of active life on the lake he had been a pilot, a deck-hand, a waiter, and a kitchen assistant on board steamers, and a sailor, helmsman, and cook on board other craft. He picked up considerable money, for a boy, by his enterprise, which, like a good son with a clear apprehension of domestic circumstances, he gave to his mother. At the time of his introduction to the reader, Lawry had just piloted a canal-boat, with movable masts, from Whitehall to Plattsburg, and was working his passage home on the "Missisque.

"Captain John feels bad about the loss of his sail," said Mr. Randall, as the sloop's boat pulled off from the shore.

"Yes, he does; but it was his own fault," replied Lawry. "He paid too much attention to his dinner at the time."

"That's true; he was very fond of the green-apple pies."

"Well, they were good," added the young pilot.

"I'm sorry he lost his sail."

"It wasn't worth much, though it was a bad time to lose it."

"He lost his temper, too. I wanted to land on the other side, but the captain was so cross I didn't like to ask him when we were so close to this shore. Your father is the ferryman, I believe."

"Yes, sir."

"Will you ask him to take me over?"

"He's going right over in the large boat, for there's a team waiting for him," replied Lawry, pointing to a horse and wagon, the owner of which had sounded the horn just as the passengers from the boat landed.

"Ask him to be as quick as possible, for I'm in a hurry," added the bank director.

"Won't you come into the house, sir?"

"No, I will sit down under this tree."

Lawry went into the house, where the family were at dinner, the meal having been delayed by the absence of the ferryman on the other side of the lake. The youth was greeted coldly by his father, and very warmly by his mother.

"I'm glad you've got home, Lawry, for Mr. Sherwood has been after you three times," said Mrs. Wilford, when the young pilot had been duly welcomed by all the family.

"What does he want?" asked Lawry.

"His little steamboat is at Port Henry, and he wants you to go up and pilot her down."

"The *Woodville?*"

"Yes, that's her name, I believe."

"Well, I'm all ready to go."

"Sit down and eat your dinner.

"I've been to dinner."

"Mr. Sherwood wanted you to go up in the *Sherman*; but it is too late for her, and he may go in the night boat."

"I'm ready when he is. Father, there is a gentleman outside who wants to go over the lake; and there is a team waiting in the road," continued Lawry.

"They must wait till I've done my dinner," replied the ferryman. "Who is the gentleman?"

"Mr. Randall; he is a director in a bank, and has six thousand dollars with him."

"I suppose so; every man but me has six thousand dollars in his pocket. Where's he going to?"

"To Shoreham, and he wants to get there by five o'clock, if he can."

"What's he traveling with so much money for?"

"I don't know. It is in his coat pocket, and it would have gone overboard if it hadn't been for me."

The ferryman finished his dinner in moody silence. He seemed to be thinking of the subject always uppermost in his mind, his thoughts stimulated, no doubt, by the fact that his expected passenger carried a large sum of money on his person.

"Mr. Randall is in a hurry, father," interposed Lawry, when the ferryman had sat a good half-hour after his son's arrival.

"He must wait till I get ready. He's got money, and I haven't; but I'm just as good as he is. I don't know why I'm poor when so many men are rich. But I'm going to be rich, somehow or other," said he, with more earnestness than he usually exhibited. "I'm too honest for my own good. I'm going to do as other men do; and I shall wake up rich some morning, as they do. Then I sha'n't have to go when folks blow the horn. They'll be willing to wait for me then."

"Don't keep the gentleman waiting, father," added Mrs. Wilford.

"I'm going to be rich, somehow or other," continued the ferryman, still pursuing the exciting line of thought he had before taken up. "I'm going to be rich, by hook or by crook."

"This making haste to get rich ruins men sometimes, husband; and haste makes waste then."

"If I can only get rich, I'll risk being ruined," said John Wilford, as he rose from the table and put on his hat.

He looked more moody and discontented than usual. Instead of hastening to do the work which was waiting for him, he stood before the window, looking out into the garden. Mrs. Wilford told him the gentleman would be impatient, and he finally left the house and walked down to the ferry-boat.

"I wonder what your father is thinking about," said Mrs. Wilford, as the door closed behind him.

"I don't know," replied Lawry; "he don't seem to be thinking that people won't wait forever for him. I guess I'll go up to Mr. Sherwood's, and see when he wants me."

"You must fix up a little before you go," replied the prudent mother. "They are very grand people up at Mr. Sherwood's, and you must look as well as you can."

"I'll put on my best clothes," added Lawry.

In half an hour he had changed his dress, and looked like another boy. Mrs. Wilford adjusted a few stray locks of his hair, and as he put on his new straw hat, and left the house, her eye followed him with a feeling of motherly pride. He was a good boy, and had the reputation of being a very smart boy, and she may be pardoned for the parental vanity with which she regarded him. While he visits the house of Mr. Sherwood, we will follow his father down to the ferry, where the bank director was impatiently waiting his appearance.

After the shower the sun had come out brightly, and the wind had abated so that there was hardly breeze enough to ruffle the waters of the lake. It was intensely warm, and Mr. Randall had taken off his coat again, but he was careful to keep it on his arm. At the approach of the ferryman he went into the boat, where he was followed by the vehicle that had been waiting so long for a passage across the lake.

John Wilford pushed off the boat with a pole, and trimmed the sail, which was the motive power of the craft when there was any wind. The ferry-boat was a large bateau, or flatboat, the slope at the ends being so gradual that a wagon could pass down over it to the bottom of the boat. This inclined plane was extended by a movable platform about six feet wide, which swung horizontally up and down, like a great trap-door. When the ferry-boat touched the shore, this platform was let down upon the ground, forming a slope on which carriages were driven into and out of the bateau.

The wind was very light, and the clumsy craft moved very slowly--so slowly that the passage promised to be a severe trial to the patience of Mr. Randall, who hoped to reach Shoreham by five o'clock. He was not in a very amiable frame of mind; he was angry at the delay in starting, and he was vexed because the wind would not blow. He walked nervously from the forward platform to the after one, with his coat still on his arm.

"We shall not get over to-night," said he impatiently, as he stopped by the side of the ferryman, and threw his coat down upon the platform, while he wiped the perspiration from his brow.

"Yes, I guess we shall," replied John Wilford.

"I'll give you a dollar if you will land me at Pointville by three o'clock."

"I can't make the wind blow, if you would give me a hundred dollars."

"Can't you use the pole or the oars?" said the bank director petulantly; "you kept me waiting half an hour before you started."

"I couldn't help that," replied John Wilford.

Mr. Randall walked to the forward platform, fretting with impatience at the indifference of the ferryman. He stood for a few moments gazing at the Vermont shore, and appeared to be engaged in estimating the distance yet to be accomplished. The calculation was not satisfactory, and the bank director's wrath was on the increase. With hasty step he walked aft again.

"I think we shall have more wind in a minute," said John Wilford, as he stepped down from the platform and adjusted the sheet.

"If we don't, I shall go crazy," replied Mr. Randall.

When he had placed one foot on the platform, by some means the drop, true to its name, went down and splashed in the water. The bank director stepped back in season to save himself from a cold bath or a watery grave, as the case might be.

"My coat! save my coat!" shouted Mr. Randall, as the garment rolled off the platform into the water.

"Why didn't you hold on to it?" said John Wilford.

"Save my coat! There is six thousand dollars in the pocket," groaned the unhappy bank director.

CHAPTER III
SIX THOUSAND DOLLARS

Within half a mile of the ferryman's cottage, at Port Rock, was the summer residence of Mr. Sherwood, who, two years before, had become the husband of Bertha Grant, of Woodville. The scenery in the vicinity was beautiful, and the mansion commanded a splendid view of the Adirondack Mountains and of the lake.

Mr. Sherwood was an enthusiastic admirer of the scenery of Lake Champlain. His constant visits at Woodville had given him a taste for aquatic sports, in which he was disposed to indulge on a larger scale than ever had been known at Woodville. He had been remarkably fortunate in his financial operations, and was already a wealthy man. Though he did not retire from active business, he had taken a partner, which enabled him to spend a part of his time during the summer at his country house on the lake.

Mr. Grant had gone to Europe a second time, to be absent during the summer, and Miss Fanny and Fanny Jane had accepted Bertha's invitation to spend a few weeks at Port Rock. A splendid time had been promised them by Mrs. Sherwood, who had made extensive preparations for their visit. The arrangements included a novelty which offered a very brilliant prospect to the party, and excited the imagination even of the older ones to the highest pitch.

This novelty was nothing less than a miniature steamboat, which had already been christened the **Woodville**, in honor of the home of the owner's lady. She was a splendid little craft, and as perfect in her machinery and appointments as any steamer that ever floated. She was a side-wheel boat, sixty feet in length, by twelve feet beam. Forward there were a regular wheel-house, a small kitchen, and other rooms usually found in a steamer. Abaft the wheels there were a saloon and two staterooms. Of course all these apartments, as well as the cabin below, were very contracted in their dimensions; but they were fitted up in the most elegant style.

The *Woodville* had cost a great deal of money; but her owner expected to realize a full return for it in the enjoyment she would afford him, his wife, and their friends. She had been sent up the Hudson, and through the canal to Whitehall, and thence to Port Henry, where she had arrived on the day before Lawry Wilford's return to Port Rock.

On board of the little steamer there is an old friend of our readers. He may be found in the engine-room; and as he rubs up the polished iron of the machinery, he is thinking of Fanny Jane Grant, with whom he escaped from the Indians in Minnesota, and whom he expects on board with Mr. Sherwood's party. The young man, now sixteen years of age, is the engineer of the *Woodville*. Though he has been but two years learning the trade of machinist, he is as thoroughly acquainted with every part of a marine-engine as though he had spent his lifetime in studying it.

The engine of the *Woodville* was built at the works where Ethan French was learning his trade, and he had been employed in its construction. As he was a frequent visitor at Woodville, he had petitioned for the situation he now held. At first, Mr. Sherwood was not willing to trust him; but Ethan's employers declared that he was a man in everything but years, and was fully competent to manage the engine, and even to build one after the designs were made. He had come up from New York in the steamer. He had seen Mr. Sherwood at Port Henry, on his arrival, and had been ordered to have the boat in readiness to start on the following morning, when the family would be passengers.

Mr. Sherwood had already selected Lawry Wilford as the pilot of the *Woodville*. He was small in stature, and would look better in the wheel-house than a full-grown man. He had often met the young pilot, and had been greatly pleased with his energy and decision. Lawry had been employed by Miss Fanny several times to row her on the lake; and he had served her so faithfully that her influence was not wanting in procuring for him the situation.

Lawry, not yet informed of the honorable and responsible position which had been awarded to him, walked up to Mr. Sherwood's house. He had heard Miss Fanny speak of the *Woodville*, while in the boat with him, and had listened with delight to her enthusiastic description of the beautiful craft. He was quite as anxious to see her as any of the party who were more directly interested in her.

"Can I see Mr. Sherwood?" asked Lawry.

"He has gone away," replied the man.

"Where has he gone?"

"To Port Henry; he went in the carriage, and is coming back in the new steamboat."

"Has he got a pilot?" continued Lawry anxiously.

"I don't know; he expected you, I believe; but when you didn't come back, he couldn't wait any longer. I heard him say he could pilot her himself, and I suppose he is going to do so."

"I'm sorry I didn't see him; I have but just got home," replied Lawry.

He wanted to pilot the beautiful little steamer up from Port Henry. He wanted to see her; wanted to make her acquaintance, for she promised to be the belle of the lake. He was sorry to lose the chance, for it might prove to be a valuable one to him. Mr. Sherwood was very liberal, and he hoped he would not engage another pilot. It was no use to complain, and Lawry walked back to the ferry, where he could see the steamer when she arrived. When he reached the landing-place, the ferry-boat was about halfway across the lake, and his attention was attracted by the strange movements of those on board of her. His father was laboring at the steering-oar with a zeal which indicated that some unusual event had occurred. The ferry-boat was thrown up into the wind, and while Lawry was waiting to ascertain what the matter was, his father leaped into the water.

It was now evident to Lawry that something serious had happened, and he sprang into the small keel-boat, used for conveying foot-passengers across the lake, which was fastened to a stake on the shore. Taking the oars, he pulled with all his might toward the ferry-boat. He was a stout boy, and handled his oars very skillfully; but before he could reach the scene of the excitement, his father had returned to the bateau.

"There's your coat," said John Wilford.

Mr. Randall seized the garment with convulsive energy, and with trembling hands felt for the pocketbook in which the six thousand dollars had been kept.

"It is gone!" gasped he; and he seemed ready to sink down in the bottom of the boat when he discovered his loss.

"Gone!" exclaimed John Wilford.

"What's the matter?" asked Lawry.

"I've lost my pocketbook with six thousand dollars in it," groaned the bank director.

"How did you lose it?" demanded Lawry.

"That drop came down and let my coat into the lake; but I don't see how my pocketbook could get out of the coat."

"I don't believe the money was in the pocket," added the ferryman.

"Yes, it was," persisted Mr. Randall.

"I don't see how it could fall out of the pocket," said John Wilford.

"Nor I; but the money is gone," answered the bank director, with a vacant stare. "I'm ruined!"

"Well, I can't help it. I've done all I could for you. I tried to save it; and if I get the rheumatism for a month or two, it will be a bad job for me."

"Wasn't the pocketbook in the pocket when you picked up the coat?" asked Mr. Randall, walking up to the ferryman.

"How should I know?" replied John Wilford. "I gave you the coat just as I found it."

"I don't believe the pocketbook would sink," added the director. "There was nothing but paper in it."

"Of course it wouldn't sink, then," interposed the owner of the vehicle in the ferry-boat.

"I don't think it would," said Mr. Randall.

"I know it wouldn't," protested the stranger. "I dropped my pocketbook into the lake once, and it floated ten minutes before I could get it again."

"Then it must be floating about on the water," added Lawry. "I will try to find it."

"I'll go with you," said Mr. Randall.

They got into the boat, and Lawry pulled about the spot where the coat had fallen into the water for half an hour without discovering the pocketbook.

"I suppose I must give it up," sighed the director.

"I'm sure it's not on the water," replied Lawry.

"Do you suppose it would sink?"

"I don't know; the gentleman in the ferry-boat says it wouldn't."

"Stop a minute, boy, and I will soon find out," continued the unfortunate loser of the money.

He took all the money and papers out of his wallet, and stuffed it with pieces of newspaper which Lawry gave him. Having thus prepared the wallet, which he said was of the same material as the lost pocketbook, he placed it on the surface of the water, holding his hand underneath to save it, in case the trial should result differently from his anticipations. It floated, and he removed his hand from under it to exhibit his confidence in the law he had tested.

"That's plain enough," said he. "My pocketbook hasn't gone to the bottom."

"It certainly has not," replied Lawry.

"Then where is it?--that's the next question."

"Are you sure it was in your pocket when you got into the ferry-boat?"

"Just as sure as I am that I sit here."

"You were very careless about your coat on board of the sloop."

"I know I was."

"I don't see how a man could throw down his coat with six thousand dollars in the pocket," said Lawry.

"I know I'm careless; but I'm so used to carrying money that I don't think much about it. I always carry it in a pocket inside of my vest," continued the director, putting his hand in the place indicated; "but this is a new vest, and hasn't any such pocket. Things don't look all right to me. Is the ferryman your father?"

"Yes, sir; he is."

"Well, the money's gone," added Mr. Randall. "We will go back to the ferry-boat."

"Did you find it?" asked John Wilford, as the bank director stepped into the bateau.

"No; but I'm certain it has not gone to the bottom."

"Where is it, then?"

"I don't know; can you tell me?"

Mr. Randall looked at the ferryman very sharply. His manner indicated that he had some suspicions.

"How can I tell you?" replied John Wilford.

"The money was in the coat pocket when you picked it up in the water-- I know it was."

"Do you mean to say I took it out?" demanded the ferryman angrily.

"If you didn't, I don't see what has become of it."

"Do you mean to accuse my father of stealing?" said Lawry indignantly.

"I don't accuse him of anything; but here are the facts, and you can all see for yourselves."

"You throw your coat down anywhere. It would have gone overboard from the sloop if I hadn't saved it; and it won't do for so careless a man as you are to accuse anybody of stealing your money," added Lawry angrily.

"Very likely you lost it out of the pocket before you got into the ferry-boat."

"Never mind him, Lawry. I haven't got his pocketbook," interposed the ferryman.

"I know you haven't, father; and it makes me mad to hear him accuse you of stealing it."

"Mr. Randall, if you think I've got your money, I want you to satisfy yourself on the point at once," continued John Wilford, turning to the director.

"I hope you haven't."

"But you think I have. Search me, then."

Greatly to the indignation of Lawry, Mr. Randall did search the ferryman; turned out his pockets, and examined every part of his wet garments. The pocketbook was not upon his person; and the loser, in spite of the laws of specific gravity, which he had just demonstrated, was almost compelled to believe that his money had gone to the bottom of the lake.

CHAPTER IV
THE STEAMER "WOODVILLE"

Mr. Randall, now that his money was lost, declared that he had no business in Shoreham, and it was useless for him to go there. The six thousand dollars belonged to his bank, and, having an opportunity to put this sum in circulation, where it would be "kept out" for several weeks, he was making this journey to accomplish the business. He facetiously remarked that it was likely to be kept out longer than was desirable.

Lawry was so sure Mr. Randall had dropped the pocketbook on the shore before he got into the ferry-boat, that he insisted upon returning to Pork Rock and having the ground searched. Though the bank director was satisfied that the pocketbook was safe in his possession when he entered the bateau, he was willing to return, since the object of his journey had been defeated, and Lawry pulled him back to the landing-place. The ground under the tree, and over which Mr. Randall had walked while waiting for the ferryman, was carefully examined, but the lost pocketbook could not be found.

The bank director had very little to say after he left the ferry-boat; but he was very thoughtful, as a man who had lost six thousand dollars might reasonably be. After the search on shore was completed, he walked off toward the village without mentioning his intentions, but he looked as though he purposed to do something.

"What's the matter, Lawry?" asked Mrs. Wilford, who had been watching the movements of Mr. Randall and her son from the window, as she came out of the house.

"The gentleman has lost his money--six thousand dollars," replied Lawry.

"Lost it!" exclaimed Mrs. Wilford, recalling the conversation with her husband at dinner.

"His coat fell overboard, and the pocketbook dropped out."

"Fell into the lake," added she, with a feeling of relief.

"Yes; father swam out and got the coat, but the money was gone."

Mrs. Wilford returned to the house. Perhaps she had some misgivings, and felt more than before that those who make haste to be rich are often ruined; but she said nothing. Lawry was perplexed at the disappearance of the money. Mr. Randall had proved that a pocketbook with nothing but paper in it would not sink within a reasonable time. If the lost treasure had fallen into the water, he would certainly have found it. If it had been dropped on shore or in the ferry-boat, it would not have disappeared so strangely.

Lawry was so positive that the pocketbook was still in the ferry-boat, or on the shore, that he renewed the search, and carefully scrutinized every foot of ground between the house and the landing-place, but with no better success than before. By this time the ferry-boat, which had been favored by a good wind during the last half-hour, returned.

"What do you suppose became of that pocketbook, father?" asked Lawry, as he stepped into the boat.

"I don't know. I don't believe he lost any pocketbook," replied John Wilford.

"He says he did, and I saw it myself."

"Perhaps you did, but I don't believe there was any six thousand dollars in it. If there had been, he wouldn't have thrown it about as he did."

"He says there was six thousand dollars in the pocketbook."

"I don't believe it. It's a likely story that a man would throw down his coat, with all that money in the pocket, on the drop. In my opinion it's some trick to cheat his creditors out of their just due."

"It don't seem possible."

"That's the truth, you may depend upon it. That's the way men make money."

Lawry was by no means satisfied with this explanation. He went into the boat, and carefully searched every part of it. His father watched him with considerable interest, declaring that it was useless to look for what had not been lost.

"You had better go up and see Mr. Sherwood now," said Mr. Wilford.

"I have been up, and he was not at home."

"You better go again, then."

"He has gone to Port Henry after the new steamer."

"Has he got a pilot?"

"Not that I know of."

"He can't get one at Port Henry," said the ferryman.

"I suppose he is going to pilot her himself."

"He will pilot her on the rocks, then. He don't know anything about Lake Champlain. Why don't you row up the lake till you meet the boat?"

"I was thinking of doing so, but I can't keep this money out of my mind."

"Why need you trouble yourself about that?" demanded the father impatiently.

"It was lost in your boat, and I am very anxious that it should be found. I'm sure Mr. Randall thinks you've got it."

"Well, he searched me, and found out that I hadn't got it--didn't he?" added Mr. Wilford, with a sickly smile.

"I don't like to have you suspected of such a thing, and for that reason I want to find the money."

"You can't find it, and I tell you he hasn't lost any money. He's going to cheat the bank or his creditors out of six thousand dollars."

"I don't believe he would do such a thing as that."

"We have looked everywhere for the money, and it can't be found. It's no use to bother any more about the matter. It's gone, and that's the end of it--if he lost it at all. You have looked all over the ferry-boat, and it isn't there. If it had been floating in the lake, you couldn't help seeing it. Now, you better take your boat and row up the lake till you meet the steamer."

"I'm going pretty soon."

"Better go now. I'm going up after a drink of water. If you don't go pretty soon, you will be too late to do any good on board the steamer," said Mr. Wilford, hoping, if he left the spot, his son would depart also.

Lawry hauled in the rowboat, ready to embark; but, before he did so, he made one more search in the bateau for the pocketbook. The timbers of the ferry-boat were ceiled over on the bottom, leaving a space for the leakage between the inner and the outer planking. Near the mast there was a well, from which, with a grain-shovel, the water was thrown out. Lawry examined this hole, feeling under the planks, and thrusting the shovel in as far as he could. This search was unavailing, and he gave it up in despair. As he stepped on shore, his curiosity prompted him to look under the platform outside of the boat.

The pocketbook was there!

In a space between the planks, a foot above the surface of the water, and the same distance from the side, the pocketbook was thrust in. It could not be seen from the inside of the boat, nor from the platform; and it could not have got there of itself.

Lawry's face turned red, and his heart bounded with emotion, for the situation of the pocketbook pointed to but one conclusion. It had been placed there by his father, who had evidently taken it from the pocket of the coat, and concealed it, either before or after the garment had fallen into the water. He was appalled and horrified at the discovery. He knew that his father was discontented with his lot; that he was indolent and thriftless; but he did not think him capable of committing a crime.

He reached under the platform, and took the pocketbook from its hiding-place. It was perfectly dry; it had not been in the water. John Wilford had probably taken it from the coat pocket, and after thrusting it into the aperture beneath the drop, had let the platform fall into the water for the purpose of dislodging the coat, and making it appear that the money had been lost in the lake.

The pocketbook seemed to burn in Lawry's fingers, and he returned it to the place where he had found it; for he was confused, and did not know what to do. He stood, with flushed face and beating heart, on the shore, considering what course he should take. He could not think of exposing his father's crime, on the one hand, or of permitting him to retain the money, on the other.

After long and painful deliberation, he decided to take the pocketbook, follow Mr. Randall, and return it to him, telling him that he had found it under the drop of the boat. He was about to adopt this course when his father came out of the house, and walked down to the ferry-boat.

"Not gone yet?" said Mr. Wilford.

"No, sir; that money has troubled me so much that I could not go," replied Lawry.

"What's the use of bothering your head about that any longer?" added the father petulantly.

"It troubles me terribly."

"Let it go; it can't be found, and that's the end of it."

"But it can be found."

"Why don't you find it, then?"

"I have found it, father!"

"What!"

"It's in a crack under the platform," replied Lawry.

"You don't mean so!" exclaimed the ferryman.

"It's no use to talk round the barn, father; the pocket-book is just where you put it."

"Where I put it? What do you mean, Lawry?"

"There it is in the crack under the drop, a foot above the water. It did not wash in there of itself. Oh, father!"

Lawry, unable longer to control his feelings, burst into tears.

"What are you crying about, Lawry? Do you think I hid the pocketbook?"

"I know you did, father," sobbed Lawry.

"Do you accuse me of stealing?" demanded Mr. Wilford, with a weak show of indignation.

"I don't accuse you of anything, father; but there it is."

"You mean to say that I stole it?"

"Oh, father!"

"Stop your whining, Lawry! What possessed you to poke round after what did not concern you? Now, shut up, and go off about your business."

"You will not keep it, father?"

"I haven't got it. If you have found it, I suppose there is time enough to think what is best to be done."

"I don't want any time to think of it," replied Lawry; and before his father could prevent him, he took the pocketbook from its place of concealment.

"What are you going to do with it?" demanded Mr. Wilford.

"I'm going to find Mr. Randall, and give it back to him, as quick as I can."

"What's the use of doing that?"

"Because it's the right way to do."

"That isn't the way to get rich."

"But it's the way to keep honest."

"Give it to me, Lawry."

"What are you going to do with it, father?"

"That's my business."

"I shall give it back to the owner."

"No, you won't, Lawry. Do you want to get me into trouble--to have me sent to jail?"

"If I give it back to Mr. Randall, there will be no trouble."

"Lawry, I've been poor and honest long enough. I'm going to do as other men do. I'm going to get rich."

"By keeping this money?" exclaimed the son.

"You needn't talk any more about it; I put the money where you found it."

"I know you did."

"Give it to me."

"I will not, father, if you mean to keep it."

"I do mean to keep it. Do you think I have run all this risk for nothing? Give me the pocketbook."

"Don't think of such a thing as keeping it, father," pleaded Lawry.

"I'm going to be rich," replied the father doggedly.

"You know what mother said about making haste to be rich: 'Haste makes waste.'"

"It will make waste if you don't give me the pocket-book."

"Mr. Randall will not be satisfied till he gets his money, and you will certainly be found out."

"No, I shall not be found out. I'll go to New York and change off the money this very night."

"But only think of it, father. You will be a thief. You never will have a moment's peace as long as you live."

"I never did have, and I shall not be any worse off," said Mr. Wilford coldly. "There comes your steamer. She hasn't got any pilot on board; I know by the way she steers. You had better go and see to her, for she is running right for the Goblins."

Lawry glanced at the **Woodville**, as she appeared rounding a point, two miles distant.

"If you will go and find Mr. Randall, I will give you the pocketbook, father," replied Lawry.

"Well, I guess you are right, Lawry, and I'll do it."

"He has gone up to the village," added Lawry, as he handed the money to his father.

CHAPTER V
HASTE AND WASTE

Lawry, satisfied that his father had come to his senses, and would restore the pocketbook to Mr. Randall, hastened into the boat, and pulled toward the *Woodville*. He was afraid Mr. Sherwood had been too venturesome in attempting to pilot the little steamer in waters with which he was entirely unfamiliar; but he hoped for the best, and rowed as hard as he could, in order to give him timely warning of the perils which lay in the path of the beautiful craft.

About half a mile above the landing at Port Rock there was a dangerous ledge, called the Goblins, some of whose sharp points were within a foot of the surface of the water when the lake was low. They were some distance from the usual track of steamers, and there was no buoy, or other mark, on them. The *Woodville* was headed toward the rocks, as the ferryman had said, and it was impossible for Lawry to get within hailing distance of her before she reached them. He pulled with all his strength, and had hoped to overhaul her in season to avert a catastrophe.

Occasionally, as he rowed, he looked behind him to observe the course of the steamer. She was almost up to the Goblins, while he was too far off to make himself heard in her wheel-house. He was appalled at her danger, and the cold sweat stood on his brow, as he saw her hastening to certain destruction. He could no longer hope to reach her, and he ceased rowing.

Standing up in his boat, he waved his hat, and made other signs to warn the imprudent pilot of his danger. With one of the oars he tried to signify to him that he must keep off; but no notice was taken of his warning. On the forward deck of the little craft stood three ladies, who, taking the boatman's energetic gestures for friendly salutations, were waving their handkerchiefs to him.

"Hard aport your helm!" shouted Lawry.

Mr. Sherwood sounded the whistle, evidently taking the shout as a cheer of congratulation at his safe arrival.

"Keep off!" roared Lawry.

Again the whistle sounded, and the ladies waved their handkerchiefs more vigorously than before. The young pilot was in despair. The *Woodville* was going at full speed directly upon the rocks, whose sharp points would grind her to powder if she struck upon them.

"Hard aport!" repeated Lawry desperately.

Once more the supposed cheer was answered by the whistle and the waving of the ladies' handkerchiefs, and still the fairy craft dashed on toward the rocks.

"By gracious! she's on them, as sure as the world!" exclaimed Lawry to himself, hardly able to breathe.

He had hardly uttered the words before he heard the crash which announced the doom of the *Woodville*. Her sharp bow slid upon the ledge, and she suddenly stopped in her mad flight.

Lawry bent on his oars again, horrified by the accident. He pulled as he had never pulled before. A moment or two after the steamer struck, he was startled by a succession of shrill shrieks from the ladies, and he turned to see what had happened. The *Woodville* had filled, rolled off the rock, and sank in deep water, leaving her passengers floating helplessly on the lake. The upper half of her smokestack was all that remained in sight of the beautiful craft which three minutes before had been a thing of beauty.

The young pilot did not pause an instant to contemplate the scene of destruction. He saw only the helpless persons struggling for life in the water, and he renewed his labors with a vigor and skill which soon brought him to the sufferers. Mr. Sherwood was supporting his wife; but both of them were nearly exhausted. Lawry helped Bertha into the boat, and told her husband to hold on at the rail.

Ethan French, with his arm around the waist of Fanny Jane, was holding on at the smokestack, where also the fireman of the boat was supporting himself.

"Where is Fanny?" gasped Mr. Sherwood.

"I'm afraid she has gone down," replied Ethan French. "I saw her just there a moment since."

"I see her!" said Lawry, as he dived into the lake.

Fanny, exhausted by her struggles, had sunk, and Lawry, with a strong arm, bore her to the surface again; but she was too large and heavy for him, and he could not support her.

Before the arrival of the boat, Ethan was in the act of transferring his helpless burden to the arms of the fireman, that he might go to the assistance of Miss Fanny; and, as soon as Lawry appeared, he swam out to help him. With the aid of the young engineer, the exhausted lady was lifted into the boat. Fanny Jane was next taken in, but there was no room for any more.

Though Miss Fanny was in a worse condition than the other ladies, she still had her senses; and none of the party was in danger. Mr. Sherwood, Ethan, and the fireman were still in the water, holding on at the rail of the boat. Lawry took the oars and pulled toward the ferry-landing.

"Thank God, we are all safe!" said Mr. Sherwood.

"Some of us must have been drowned if Lawry had not come to our assistance," added Miss Fanny. "I had given up, and was sinking to the bottom. My senses were leaving me, when I felt his grasp on my arm."

"You have done bravely, Lawry," added Bertha.

But the party did not feel much like talking. They were all grateful to God, who had, through the agency of the young pilot, saved them from their perilous situation. When the boat reached the landing-place, the ladies were conducted to the cottage of John Wilford, where everything was done by Mrs. Wilford to promote their comfort. Lawry hastened up to Mr. Sherwood's house to procure the carriage, which had fortunately just returned from Port Henry, and the party were soon conveyed to their home.

Dry clothing and a little rest soon restored Mr. Sherwood and the ladies to their wonted spirits, and all of them wished to see their brave deliverer. He was sent for, and presented himself to the ladies in the drawing-room. Lawry, anxious to learn the condition of the ladies after their cold bath, and their terrible fright, had followed the carriage up to the house, and was telling the coachman the particulars of the catastrophe when he was summoned to the presence of the family.

Never was a young man more earnestly and sincerely thanked for a brave and noble deed; and Mr. Sherwood hinted that something more substantial than thanks would be bestowed upon him.

"Thank you, sir; I don't need anything more," replied Lawry, blushing. "What will be done with the steamer, now?" he asked.

"I have got enough of her," said Mr. Sherwood. "She has given me a shock I shall never forget."

"I don't think it was the fault of the boat, sir," suggested Lawry. "I did all I could to have you keep off the rocks."

"We all thought you were crazy, you shook so in your boat."

"I was trying to warn you of your danger."

"Was that what you meant? We thought you were cheering the *Woodville*."

"I saw you were going on the rocks, and I shouted and made signs for you to keep off."

"You certainly did all you could for us, both before and after the accident," added Mr. Sherwood. "When did you get home, Lawry?"

"To-day noon, just after you went to the house for me. I came right up to see you; but I found you had gone."

"Yes; I was so impatient to get that little steamer up here, that I couldn't wait any longer."

"And what a waste your haste has made!" laughed Mrs. Sherwood. "There is our fine little steamer at the bottom of the lake."

"She may lie there, for all me," added Mr. Sherwood.

"I should not dare to put my foot on board of her again," said Miss Fanny.

"Nor I," chimed in Fanny Jane.

"She isn't to blame, Mr. Sherwood," interposed Ethan French. "She worked as though she had been alive."

"No steamer could stand such a thump on the Goblins," added Lawry.

"I don't blame the boat, of course," replied Mr. Sherwood; "but this adventure has cured me of my love for steamboating. I don't want to see another one."

"Shall you let the *Woodville* lie there?" asked Lawry.

"She's a wreck now, stove in and ruined."

"But she can be raised and repaired, and be as good as ever, or nearly so," continued Lawry.

"She is good for nothing to me now. I will give her to any one who wants her."

"There are plenty who will want her," said Lawry.

"It will cost them a fortune to raise and repair her--almost as much as she is worth, if she is to be used as a plaything. But I have come to the conclusion that she is a dangerous machine for me, and I don't want anything more to do with her. I came very near drowning my wife and my friends with her; and this fills me with disgust for the boat and for myself."

"Just now you spoke of a reward for what I had the good luck to do for you, Mr. Sherwood," continued Lawry.

"I did; and you may be assured I shall never forget your noble conduct," replied Mr. Sherwood warmly.

"If you are going to give the *Woodville* away, sir--"

"Well, what?" asked Mr. Sherwood, as the young pilot paused.

"I don't know as I ought to say what I was going to say."

"Say it, Lawry, say it," added Mr. Sherwood kindly.

"You said you would give the steamer to any one who wanted her," continued Lawry, hesitating.

"And you want her?" laughed the wealthy gentleman.

"Yes, sir; that is what I was going to say."

"Then she is yours, Lawry; but I might as well give you the fee simple of a farm in Ethiopia. I don't feel as though I had given you anything, my boy."

"Indeed you have, sir! I feel as though you had made my fortune for me; and I am very much obliged to you, sir."

"I don't believe you have anything to thank me for, Lawry. As I understand it, the *Woodville* lies on the bottom of the lake, with her bow stove in, and her hull as useless as though the parts had never been put together. The engine and the iron and brass work are worth a good deal of money, I know; but it will cost all they will bring to raise them."

"I don't think the steamer is ruined, sir. I hope you are not giving her away believing that she is not worth anything," said Lawry.

"I don't think she is worth much."

"I think she stove a great hole in her bow, and that is all that ails her. If we can get her on the ways, she can be made as good as ever she was in a week."

"Whatever her condition, Lawry, she is yours. I will give you a bill of sale of her at once."

Mr. Sherwood executed the paper in due form, affixed the stamp, and gave the document to the young pilot.

"I can hardly help weeping when I think of the beautiful little steamer," said Mrs. Sherwood. "She was a perfect little fairy. How elated we were as we moved up the lake in her! What fine times we were promising ourselves on board of her! Now the dear little craft lies on the bottom of the lake, broken and spoiled!"

"I shouldn't dare to put my foot in her again," added Miss Fanny. "I shudder when I think of her."

"I shudder when I think of you, Fanny. You were sinking when Lawry dived down after you," said Mr. Sherwood.

"We ought all to be grateful to God for His mercy in saving us," added Fanny Jane.

"I trust we are grateful to Him; and I am sure we shall never forget what Lawry has done to-day," responded the gentleman.

"Never!" exclaimed Fanny warmly.

"It was all my fault," continued Mr. Sherwood. "I am ashamed of myself, and disgusted with the boat."

"The boat is not to blame, sir," said Ethan French. "She behaved like a lady."

"I know she is not to blame. It was my silly impatience. I was in such a hurry to try the steamer that I could not wait for a pilot. Bertha, do you know what your father used to say to me when I was in a hurry?"

"I don't know; but I have heard him say that you were too impatient for your own good."

"'Haste and Waste' was his maxim, when I was not disposed to wait the natural development of events. By neglecting this precept, I have nearly sacrificed the lives of my best friends. Lawry, if you are going to be a steamboat man, let me give you this maxim for your government--'Haste and Waste.'"

CHAPTER VI
THE SHERIFF'S VISIT

Lawry put the bill of sale of the *Woodville* in his pocket, and felt like a steamboat proprietor; for the fact that his steamer lay at the bottom of the lake did not seem to lessen her value. She was in a safe place, and there was no danger of her "blowing up" or drifting away from him. The haste of Mr. Sherwood had been "a windfall" to him, though Lawry would not willingly have purchased the steamer at the peril of so many precious lives. He was ready to accept the moral and prudential deductions from the catastrophe, and really believed that the rich man's maxim was a safe and valuable one.

In his own limited experience, Lawry could recall many instances where haste had made waste; but the foolish conduct of Mr. Sherwood in attempting to navigate the *Woodville* in water with which he was totally unacquainted was the most impressive example of the worth of the proverb, and he felt that the steamer, in his own possession, would always mean "haste and waste" to him.

"I have often heard my father speak of the folly of unconsidered action and blind haste," said Bertha. "He lost a valued friend in the steamship *Arctic*, which was sunk, and hundreds of lives sacrificed, by running at full speed in a dense fog. In her case, haste was not only a terrible waste of property, but of life."

"That will be worth remembering, Lawry, when you are in command of a steamer," added Mr. Sherwood.

"I don't think I ever shall be in such a position," replied Lawry modestly.

"I am afraid you never will be on board of the *Woodville*."

"I'm pretty sure she can be raised, though I may not have the means to do it myself," continued Lawry.

"You shall have all the means you want, my boy," replied Mr. Sherwood. "We owe you a debt of gratitude which we shall never be able to pay, and if you want anything, don't fail to call upon me."

"If you need any help, Lawry, I'm with you," said Ethan French.

"Thank you; I dare say I shall want all the help I can get," answered Lawry, as he took his leave of the family.

"I'm the owner of a steamboat!" thought he. "I'm a lucky fellow, and I shall make my fortune in the *Woodville*. I can take out parties, or I can run her on a day route from Burlington up the lake; and there is towing enough to keep me busy all summer."

Excited by the brightest visions of the future, he came in sight of his father's cottage. It looked poorer and meaner than it had ever looked before; and perhaps he thought it was hardly a fit abode for a steamboat proprietor. When he saw the tall mast of the ferry-boat, with the sail flapping idly in the wind, he was reminded of the events which had occurred on board of her that afternoon. It was mortifying to think that his father had even been tempted to steal; but he was rejoiced to know that he had been induced to return the six thousand dollars to the owner.

Lawry had not seen his father since he left the landing-place to board the *Woodville*. He was not at the house when the party landed, after the catastrophe, and Lawry was glad he was not there, for his absence assured the anxious son that he had gone in search of Mr. Randall. Amid the exciting events which had followed the painful discovery that his father intended to steal the six thousand dollars, the young pilot had not thought of the matter, for his mind was entirely relieved by Mr. Wilford's promise to give up the money.

Lawry went into the house; his father had not yet returned, and his mother asked him a hundred questions about the steamboat disaster, as she set the table for supper. When the meal was ready, Mrs. Wilford went to the door and blew a tin horn, which was intended to summon the ferryman to his tea.

"I think father has not got back yet," said Lawry.

"Where has he gone?"

"Up to the village, I believe," replied Lawry, who had determined not to tell his mother of the great temptation to which his father had almost yielded.

"What has he gone up there for?" inquired Mrs. Wilford, who perhaps saw in the anxious looks of her son that something had been concealed from her.

"He had a little business up there," answered the young pilot. "I think we had better not wait for him, for he may not be back for some time. I haven't shown you this paper, mother," he continued, wishing to draw off her attention from his father, as he handed her the bill of sale of the **Woodville**, and seated himself at the table.

"What is it, Lawry?"

"It is a bill of sale of the little steamer."

"A what?" demanded Mrs. Wilford, as she paused with the teapot suspended over a cup.

"A bill of sale of the new steamer."

"What, the one that was sunk?"

"Yes; Mr. Sherwood has given her to me, just as she lies."

"Humph! He might as well have given you a five-acre lot at the bottom of the lake. What in the world can you do with a steamboat smashed to pieces and sunk?"

"I can raise her."

"You may as well think of raising the Goblins on which she sank."

"She can be raised, mother."

"Perhaps she can, but you can't raise her."

"I shall try, at any rate," replied Lawry confidently.

The conversation was interrupted by the arrival of the ferryman. The son cast an anxious glance at his father, as the latter took his accustomed place at the table. A forced smile played about the lips of Mr. Wilford; but Lawry interpreted it as an effort to overcome the sense of humiliation his father must feel at having his dishonest intentions discovered by his son.

"Well, Lawry, I found him," said Mr. Wilford.

"Did you? I'm very glad you did," replied the son.

"Who?" asked Mrs. Wilford.

"The bank man--the one that lost the money," replied the ferryman.

"What did you want of him?"

"We found his money after he had gone."

"Did you? I'm so glad! And neither of you said a word to me about it."

"I gave it back to him, and it's all right now."

Unhappily, it was not all right; and the ferryman had scarcely uttered the words before a knock was heard at the door. Without awaiting the movements of Mrs. Wilford, who rose from the table to open the door, the visitors entered. Mr. Wilford turned deadly pale, for the first person that passed the threshold was the sheriff, whose face was familiar to the ferryman. He was followed by Mr. Randall and a constable.

Lawry's heart sank within him when he saw who the visitors were. He feared that his father, in spite of his statement to the contrary, had been led to appropriate the six thousand dollars. It was a moment of agony to him, and he would have given his right, title, and interest in the sunken steamer for the assurance that his parent was an honest man.

"I come on rather unpleasant business, Mr. Wilford," the sheriff began; "but I suppose I may as well speak out first as last."

"Goodness! what can you want here!" exclaimed Mrs. Wilford.

"Don't be alarmed, Mrs. Wilford," said the sheriff. "It may be all right, for what I know. Mr. Randall, here, has lost a large sum of money, and he thinks he has been robbed. I'm sure I hope it's all right."

"Why, husband!" ejaculated Mrs. Wilford; "didn't you just say--"

"I didn't say anything," interposed the ferryman.

Lawry was quite as pale as his father. He would rather have been accused of the crime himself than had it charged upon his father; he would rather have gone to prison himself than had him dragged away on such an infamous accusation. The sheriff's encouraging words that it might be all right, had no force or comfort for him. Lawry knew that his father was guilty, and he was in despair.

Mrs. Wilford had only heard that the money was lost, at first; and then, from her husband, that it had been found and restored to the owner. It was plain that he had told her a falsehood; that if he had found the money, it was still in his possession. The case was too plain to need much reflection. Mr. Randall and the sheriff knew less than the ferryman, less than his wife and his son; but in the good woman's estimation, it was far worse to be guilty than it was to be detected.

It would be difficult to fathom the motives which induced John Wilford to tell his wife and son that the money had been restored to the owner. Perhaps he had some plan by which he hoped to escape detection and punishment for his crime;

or it may be that he told the falsehood to satisfy Lawry for the present moment. His calculations, whatever they may have been, were exceedingly stupid and ill digested. There was an utter want of skill and judgment in his operations. He was not a strong-minded man, and his guilt seemed to have paralyzed his weak faculties. His failure to be rich in the path of dishonesty was even more signal than his honest but weak efforts in a legitimate business.

"What did he just say?" asked the sheriff, whose attention was attracted by Mrs. Wilford's words, but more by the sharp manner of her husband as he interrupted her.

"What is your business with me?" demanded the ferryman of the sheriff, earnestly.

"What did he say?" repeated the sheriff.

"If my husband has been doing anything wrong, I'm sorry for it," replied Mrs. Wilford.

"Mr. Randall thinks he has taken his money," added the sheriff. "If you can tell me what your husband just said, it might throw some light on the matter."

"Oh, husband!" cried the poor wife, throwing herself into a chair and weeping bitterly.

"Mr. Randall knows I haven't taken his money," protested the ferryman stoutly.

"Don't cry, marm," said the sheriff, moved by the distress of the afflicted wife. "Nothing has been proved yet, and for all I know, your husband may be as honest as any man in Essex County."

"I've always been an honest man, and I always expect to be," added the culprit. "I haven't got the money. If any of you think I have, why don't you do something about it--not try to frighten my wife?"

Mr. Wilford was searched by the sheriff and constable, but the money was not upon his person. The house was then carefully examined, but with no different result.

"Do you know anything about this business, Lawry?" said the sheriff, when the search was completed.

"I don't think he had anything to do with it," interposed Mr. Randall. "The boy helped me look for the pocketbook, and behaved very handsomely; but I didn't like the looks of his father."

"What did your father say just before we came?" asked the sheriff.

Lawry was stupefied with grief and shame. He knew not what to say, and he dropped his head upon the table, and sobbed like a little child.

"Things look bad, Mr. Wilford. Your wife and Lawry know more than they are willing to tell," continued the officer.

"You have scared them half out of their wits," replied the ferryman, trying to smile.

"It isn't likely we can find out anything here," said the constable. "If he has got the money, he has hid it round the house somewhere."

Adopting this suggestion, the officers, followed by Mr. Randall, left the cottage to examine the vicinity. The constable was a shrewd man, and for a country locality, quite distinguished as a thief- taker. The shower early in the afternoon had left the ground in condition to receive the tracks of every individual who had been near the ferry.

The sharp officer examined all the marks in the earth, and finally followed the footsteps of John Wilford, through a corn-field, above the cottage.

Mrs. Wilford and Lawry wept as though their hearts would break, while the ferryman, trembling with apprehension, paced the kitchen.

"What are you crying for?" said he impatiently.

"Oh, John!" sobbed his wife.

"Nothing has been proved."

"Yes, there has. You told me you had given the money to Mr. Randall."

"You told me you would restore it to the owner, when I gave you the pocket-book," added Lawry.

"Lawry, if you say a word about it, you shall go to jail with me," said Mr. Wilford angrily.

CHAPTER VII
"THE FERRYMAN'S CRIME"

Mr. Wilford, in spite of his faults and peculiarities, was a kind father, and never before had been heard to utter such terrible words as those which had just passed his lips. It was a consolation to Lawry and his mother to believe that the words were only a threat which was never intended to be executed, and only made to awe the youth into silence. It was needless; for, right or wrong, the son would have died rather than betray his father.

John Wilford's operations in hiding the money were as transparent as his efforts to quiet the suspicions of his family. The constable followed his tracks in the soft ground of the corn-field till he came to a stump in one corner of the lot. It was decayed and hollow, and in one of the cavities the pocketbook was discovered. Mr. Randall laughed for joy when it was handed up to him. Its contents were undisturbed, and not a dollar of the money was missing. The party walked back to the house, having been absent less than half an hour. The ferryman was just coming out as they entered the gate.

"I hope you are satisfied," said he, confident that the officers would never think of crossing the corn-field in search of the lost treasure.

"I'm satisfied, Mr. Wilford," said the sheriff.

"Don't you think it is a mean thing to come here and accuse me of robbing one of my passengers?" continued the ferryman.

"I don't think so."

"In my opinion, Mr. Randall hasn't lost any money. I don't believe a man would throw his coat down anywhere if there was six thousand dollars in the pocket."

"But the money was lost, whether you believe it or not," interposed the bank director, irritated by this charge.

"I've heard of such a thing as men losing money to cheat their creditors, or something of that sort," added the ferryman.

"Don't talk so, husband," said Mrs. Wilford, who, with Lawry, had come out of the house when they heard the voice of the sheriff, anxious to learn the result of the search.

"Don't you think that's mean, to accuse a man of cheating his creditors, after you have stolen his money?" retorted Mr. Randall.

"What right have you to say I stole your money?" demanded Mr. Wilford, with a show of intense indignation.

"Because you did."

"Can you prove it?"

"I think I can."

"No, you can't. I don't believe you lost any money. It's only a trick to cheat the bank or your creditors."

"We shall see."

"Don't talk so, husband," repeated Mrs. Wilford.

"Keep still, wife. When a man hasn't done anything, it's hard to be charged with stealing six thousand dollars. They can't prove anything."

"Yes, we can, Mr. Wilford," interposed the sheriff. "It becomes my duty to arrest you, though I would rather have done it when your family were not present."

"Arrest me! What for?" exclaimed John Wilford. "You can't prove anything."

"Yes, we can," replied the sheriff.

"What can you prove?"

"I think it would be better for you not to talk so much," added the sheriff, in a low tone. "Come with me, and I will do my duty as quietly as possible."

"Come with you! What for?" said Mr. Wilford, in a loud tone. "I didn't steal the money."

"It's a plain case. It's no use for you to deny it any longer."

"But I didn't."

"We have found the money, just where you put it."

"Found--what!" stammered the guilty man.

"Oh, husband!" groaned Mrs. Wilford.

"Oh, father!" sobbed Lawry.

"I'm sorry, Mrs. Wilford," said the kind-hearted officer; "but it's all as plain as daylight. He took the money and hid it in a stump in the corn-field, where we found it."

"What shall we do?" cried Mrs. Wilford.

"It's a bad business, marm, but I can't help it. I must do my duty."

Mr. Wilford leaned on the garden-fence, with his gaze fixed upon the ground. He could not look the loved ones in the face, after the crime he had committed. The smaller children, who had been at play around the house, were now gathered about the group, unable fully to comprehend the terrible misfortune which had befallen them; though, as they gazed on Lawry and their mother, they could not help realizing that something very sad had happened.

"I'm ready to go with you," said John Wilford to the sheriff, for the scene was too affecting and humiliating.

"Oh, husband, why did you do it?" exclaimed Mrs. Wilford, as she grasped one of his arms, clinging to him like a true woman, in spite of his shame and infamy.

"I don't know why I did it. I was crazy. I wanted to be rich," replied the unhappy man.

"I wish you had given back the money, as you said you did."

"I wish I had now."

"Can nothing be done?" continued Mrs. Wilford, appealing to the sheriff. "Must he go with you?"

"He must; my duty is as plain as it can be."

The poor woman suggested various expedients to avoid the fearful consequences; she appealed to the bank director, and begged him not to prosecute her husband. Mr. Randall, though he had been greatly irritated by the cruel insinuations of the culprit, was not a malignant man; and he was disposed to grant the petition of the disconsolate wife. He had recovered his money, and had no malice against the ferryman. But the sheriff declared that no such arrangement could be tolerated. The matter had been placed in his hands, and, as a sworn officer of the law, he should be obliged to arrest the offender.

In vain Mrs. Wilford pleaded for her husband; in vain Lawry pleaded for his father; the sheriff, kind and considerate as he had shown himself to be, was inexorable in the discharge of his duty. There was no alternative; and John Wilford must go to jail. The poor wife, when she found that her tears and her pleadings were unavailing, submitted to the stern necessity. She insisted that her husband should be allowed to change his dress, which the sheriff readily granted; and in a short time the culprit appeared in his best clothes. It was a sad parting between him and his family, and even the ferryman wept as he passed out from beneath his humble roof, not again to come beneath its friendly shelter for many, many weary months.

Mrs. Wilford and Lawry were stunned by the heavy blow. The light of earthly joys seemed suddenly to have gone out, and left them in the gloom and woe of disgrace. There was nothing to be said at such a time, and they sobbed in silence, until the sound of the ferry-horn roused Lawry from his lethargy of grief. Some one wished to cross the lake, and had given the usual signal with the tin horn, placed on a post for the purpose, at the side of the road.

"There is no ferryman here now," said Mrs. Wilford gloomily.

"I will go, mother," replied Lawry.

"It may be many a day before your father comes back," added Mrs. Wilford, as she wiped away her tears. "It is a great deal worse than a funeral."

"We can't help it, mother, and I suppose we must make the best of it."

"I suppose we must; but I don't know what we are going to do."

"We shall do well enough, mother. I will attend to the ferry; but poor father--"

Lawry, finding he could not speak without a fresh flow of tears, hastened out of the house. There were two wagons waiting for him; and when they were embarked in the boat, he pushed off, and trimmed the sail for the gentle breeze that was blowing up the lake. The passengers asked for his father; but Lawry could only tell them that he had gone away: the truth was too painful for him to reveal. He returned to his desolate home when he had ferried the wagons over the lake. There was nothing but misery in that humble abode, and but little sleep for those who were old enough to comprehend the sadness and shame of their situation.

Before morning the news of John Wilford's crime had been circulated through the village of Port Rock and its vicinity. Some knew that the ferryman was lazy and thriftless, and wondered he had not robbed somebody before. Others had always regarded him as a person of no sagacity or forethought, but did not think he would steal. Many pitied his family, and some said that Lawry was "as smart as two of his father," and that his mother and the children would be well provided for.

The intelligence went to the mansion of Mr. Sherwood, and there it touched the hearts of true friends. Though none of them knew much about the ferryman and his family, yet for Lawry's sake they were deeply interested in them.

After breakfast Mr. Sherwood went down to the ferry-house; and the young pilot, with many tears and sobs, told him the whole of the sad story of his father's crime. The rich man was full of sympathy, but nothing could be done. He volunteered to be the culprit's bail, and to provide him with the best counsel in the State. But John Wilford was guilty, and nothing could wipe out this terrible truth.

Mr. Sherwood did all he had promised to do; but the ferryman, after he had been examined and fully committed for trial, declined to furnish bail, declaring that he did not wish to be seen at Port Rock again. At the next session of the court, two months after his committal, he pleaded guilty of the robbery and was sentenced to three years' imprisonment in the penitentiary at Sing Sing.

After the sentence the prisoner was permitted to see his family for the last time for many months. It was a sad and touching interview; but from it Lawry and his mother derived much consolation. John Wilford was penitent; he was truly sorry for what he had done, and declared that, when he had served out his time, he would be a better man than he had ever been before. It was comforting to the mother and son to know that the wanderer was not hardened and debased by his crime and the exposure; and they returned to their home submissive to their lot, sad and dreary as it was.

From the day his father had been arrested, Lawry felt that the care of the family devolved upon him. His older brother was away from home, and was indolent and dissipated. The ferry and the little farm must be cared for, as from them came the entire support of his mother and his brothers and sisters. Though he was oppressed by the burden of sorrow which his father's crime cast upon him, he did not yield to despair.

Half a mile below the ferry-landing he could see the smokestack of the **Woodville** projecting above the water. She was his property; and if she had seemed to be a prize to him before the calamity had fallen upon his father's household, she was doubly so now. As he crossed the ferry, he gazed up at the Goblins, with less of exultation, but more of hope, than before. In his opinion, as he expressed it to his mother, there was "money in her." Mrs. Wilford was in great tribulation lest the man who now held the mortgage upon the little farm should insist upon being paid, as there was now no hope that, the debtor, in prison, would be able to do anything. Lawry told her that the steamboat would enable them to pay all claims upon his father.

Mrs. Wilford had but little confidence in her son's schemes, but she did not discourage them; and Lawry racked his brain for expedients to accomplish the task he had imposed upon himself. He had no money, and he was too proud to ask Mr. Sherwood for the assistance which that gentleman would so gladly have rendered. Ethan French came down to see him every day, and the prairie boy was so kind and considerate that they soon became fast friends.

"When are you going to work on the steamer, Lawry?" asked Ethan. "I suppose you don't feel much like meddling with her yet."

"I don't; but she ought to be raised as soon as possible," replied Lawry. "I am going to work upon her right off. I went down to see how she lies this morning, and I have got my plans all laid."

"Have you?"

"I have."

"Do you think you can get her up?"

"I know I can."

"Well, how are you going to do it?" inquired Ethan.

"Do you know Mr. Nelson, over at Pointville? I suppose you don't. Well, he is a great oil man; he has got some oil-wells down on the St. Johns River. He is getting together all the barrels and hogsheads he can find, to send down to his works. He has as many as a hundred at his place in Pointville. I'm going to borrow a lot of these casks, if I can, and raise the *Woodville* with them."

"How are you going to manage with them?" asked Ethan, deeply interested in the plan.

"Sink them round the boat, and fasten them to her hull, till there is enough to float her."

"But how are you going to sink them?"

"There's some one to go over the ferry," replied Lawry, as a blast of the tin horn was heard. "If you will go over with me, I will tell you all about it, and we will call and see Mr. Nelson while we are at Pointville."

Ethan embarked with his friend, and when the boat started the subject was resumed.

CHAPTER VIII
RAISING THE "WOODVILLE"

Ethan French, during the two years he had been a resident of the State of New York, had been an earnest and diligent student. His mind was even more improved than his manners. His taste for mechanics had prompted him to study the various subjects included in this science, and as he stood by his companion, the pilot, he talked quite learnedly about the specific gravity of wood and iron, about displacement, buoyancy, and similar topics.

"The hull of the steamer--that is, the woodwork--will not float itself, but it will sustain considerable additional weight," said he.

"Yes, I understand all that," replied Lawry. "If there had been no iron in the *Woodville* she would not have gone down."

"The iron in her engines is seven or eight times as heavy as the same bulk of water. Its weight carried the hull down with it."

"Then we must put down empty casks enough to float the engine," added Lawry.

"No; the woodwork of the hull will hold up a portion of the weight of the engine, and we must furnish buoyancy enough to sustain the rest of it."

"It will not take a great many casks, then--will it?"

"Not a great many; but the difficulty is to get them down to the bottom, and fasten them to the hull."

"I can do that," replied Lawry confidently.

Ethan approved the method, and promised to ascertain what weight each of the casks would sustain in the water, when he had obtained their dimensions. The ferry-boat reached the other side of the lake, and the young men went to see Mr. Nelson, the owner of the casks. He did not wish to use the hogsheads till October, and was willing they should be employed for the purpose indicated, if Lawry would give him security for their safe return.

"Mr. Sherwood will do that for you, Lawry," said Ethan.

"That's a good name," added the oil speculator. "If he will guarantee the safe return of the casks, that is all I ask. I wonder if Mr. Sherwood don't want some shares in the Meteor Oil Company."

"I don't know; I'll ask him," replied Ethan.

"If you will, I won't charge you anything for the use of the casks," added Mr. Nelson.

Mr. Sherwood was consulted in the evening. He was very willing to furnish the required security for the use of the oil-casks, but he did not seem to have the same confidence in the "Meteor" which Mr. Nelson exhibited, though he promised to consider the matter.

It required three days to complete the preparations for raising the **Woodville**. All the ropes and rigging in the neighborhood, including many hay-ropes and clothes-lines, had been collected; the oil-casks had been conveyed over the lake in the ferry-boat, and secured within a "boom" composed of four long timbers, lashed together at the ends, forming a square, which was moored close to the Goblins; and a raft had been built, upon which the operations were to be conducted.

Mr. Sherwood had offered to furnish as many men as could be employed to assist in the work; but the young engineers had so arranged their plans that no help was needed. At sunrise in the morning the boys ran down to the Goblins in the ferry-boat, which was necessary for the transportation of sundry heavy articles. The raft was already there, moored in the proper place for commencing the labors of the day. The engineers were deeply interested in the operations before them, for there was a difficult problem to be solved, which required all their skill and ingenuity; and Lawry felt that his future prosperity and happiness depended upon the success of the undertaking.

Their plans and their machinery were yet to be tried, and there was a degree of excitement attending the execution of the project which was as agreeable as it was stimulating to their enthusiastic natures. People had laughed at the idea of two boys raising a steamer burdened with heavy machinery, and both of them felt that their reputations were at stake.

"Now, Lawry, we shall soon find out what we can do," said Ethan, as they made fast the ferry-boat to the raft.

"I know what we can do," replied the young pilot confidently. "If the casks will float her, she shall come to the top of the water before to-morrow night. Now, Ethan, the first thing is to get a rope under her."

"That's easy enough."

"It's all easy enough, if you only believe in yourself."

A rope of six fathoms in length was selected from the mass of rigging on the raft, and a stone just heavy enough to sink the line attached to the middle of it. Lawry took it in the wherry, sculled to the stern of the sunken steamer, and dropped it into the water. He then carried one end to Ethan, on the raft, while he returned with the other in his boat, which he moored to the opposite side of the *Woodville*. The middle of the rope was kept on the bottom of the lake by the stone, while the two ends were carried forward by the boys until the bight was drawn under the keel of the steamer, as far as her position on the rocks would permit it to go. Lawry's end was made fast around the smokestack, and Ethan's to the raft.

One of the hogsheads was next floated out of the boom enclosure, and hauled upon the raft, Lawry adjusted the hogshead slings to the cask. In the middle of the raft an aperture had been left, large enough for a hogshead to pass through, over which a small derrick had been built. A stone post, about the length of the casks, and just heavy enough to sink one of them, had been brought down on the bateau. This "sinker," as the young engineers called it, had been weighed, and it exactly conformed to the requirement of Ethan's figures; it was just sufficient to overcome the flotage power of the cask.

"Now, keep cool, Ethan, and we shall find out whether your figures are correct, or not," said Lawry.

"Figures won't lie," replied Ethan; "I know they are correct, and that hogshead will go to the bottom as quick as though it were made of lead."

"We shall soon see," added Lawry, as he placed a couple of skids across the "well." "Now we must place the sinker on those skids."

By the aid of the derrick, which was provided with a rude windlass, constructed by Ethan, the stone post was hoisted up, and then dropped down on the skids. The sinker had been rigged with slings, and the hogshead was attached to it by a contrivance of Lawry, upon which the success of the operation wholly depended, and which it will be very difficult to describe with words. The sinker would carry the cask to the bottom of the lake, where its buoyancy was to assist in bringing the steamer to the surface of the water; but it was necessary, after the cask had been sunk and fastened to the hull, to detach it from the sinker; and this had been a problem of no little difficulty to Lawry, who managed the nautical part of the enterprise.

Fastened to the slings on the sinker was a rope ten fathoms in length. A loop was formed in this line, close to the sinker, and the bight passed through the slings on the hogshead. The loop was then laid over the two ropes, one of which was fast to the sinker, and the other was the unattached end of the line, and "toggled" on with a marline-spike. If the young reader does not quite understand the process, let him take a string, with one end fastened to a flatiron; double it, and pass the loop- -which sailors call a **bight**-- upward between the thumb and forefinger; bring the loop down to meet the two parts of the string on the palm of the hand; then take the two lines into the loop, and put a pencil under the two parts drawn through the loop. The flatiron will correspond to the stone sinker, and the thumb to the slings on the hogshead. Lift up the flatiron, so that the weight will bear on the thumb; then pull out the pencil, and the iron will drop.

The marlinespike was thoroughly greased, and a small line attached to the head of it, so that it could be easily drawn out of the loop, when the cask had been secured to the hull of the steamer.

"There, we are all right now," said Lawry, after he had tried the marlinespike several times to satisfy himself that it could be easily drawn from its place. "Now we will make fast the rope which runs under the keel to the hogshead."

"Here it is," added Ethan.

"We want to have the cask under the guard of the steamer when we get it down."

"That will be easy enough."

"Perhaps it will; but I'm afraid the rope will bind on the keel."

"If it does, we must take the raft round to the other side of the **Woodville**, and pass it round the windlass; we can haul it up in that way."

"That will take too much time. I think you and I both will be strong enough to haul the cask into place."

"Now, give us a turn at the windlass, Ethan," said Lawry, when he was ready.

"Aye, aye," replied Ethan, as he turned the crank, and raised the sinker and the cask, so that the skids which supported them could be removed.

"Lower away!" added Lawry, highly excited; and the sinker began to descend into the water, carrying with it the hogshead. "That works first-rate. Now hold on till I get hold of the other end of the guide-rope."

Lawry jumped into the wherry, and sculled round to the other side of the sunken steamer, where he detached the end of the line passing under the keel from the smoke-stack, where it had been secured. He hauled on the rope till he got it clear of the stone with which it had been sunk.

"Lower away!" shouted Lawry.

"Lower, it is," answered Ethan.

"Slowly," added the pilot, as he hauled in the rope.

"It is going to the right place. I can see it in the water."

"Hold on!" cried Lawry; and the wherry was so unsteady beneath him that it was with great difficulty he "kept what he had got" on the rope.

In order to overcome this disadvantage he passed the rope around the smoke-stack.

"I have it now!" shouted he. "This gives me a splendid purchase;" and he hauled in the rope, bringing the hogshead chock up to the hull of the sunken craft.

"We are growing wiser every moment," laughed Ethan.

"So we are. Lower away, slowly. That's it," said Lawry. "Lower away."

"The sinker is on the bottom," replied Ethan.

"All right; can you see the hogshead?"

"Yes; you have hauled it completely under the guard. The water is as clear as crystal," answered Ethan.

"Hold on a moment till I make fast this line!"

Thus far the experiment had been entirely successful, and Lawry's bosom bounded with emotion. The plan for raising the **Woodville** was his own, though he had been greatly assisted by Ethan, who had designed and constructed the derrick and windlass, thus diminishing the labor of the enterprise. The young pilot felt like a conqueror when he had placed the first cask in position.

Sculling the wherry back to the raft, he pulled the string attached to the toggle, and drew it out of the noose.

"Hoist away," said he.

"Hoist, it is," replied Ethan, as he took hold with him.

"All right!" shouted the young nautical engineer. "I feel like giving three cheers," he added.

"So do I; and we'll do it, when we get the sinker on the raft."

The stone post came up "in good order and condition," and the skids were placed under it, to keep it in position for the sinking of the second hogshead. The three cheers were given with a will, and they came from the hearts of the boys. They had labored patiently for three days in gathering the material and constructing the machinery for the raising of the steamer, and their first success was a real joy.

"Breakfast-time," said Lawry, as the horn sounded from the ferry-house.

"I don't want any breakfast," answered Ethan. "I don't feel as though we could spare the time for eating."

"Haste and waste," added Lawry, laughing. "We have got a great deal of hard work to do, and we must keep our strength. For my part, I'm hungry."

"I'm not; and I'm so interested in this job that I don't like to leave. We ought to have brought our breakfast down with us."

"I don't think we shall make anything by driving the work too hard. We must keep cool, and do it well. Besides, I'm liable to be called off a dozen times a day."

"What for?"

"To take people over the ferry."

"Oh, bother!" exclaimed Ethan impatiently. "Have we got to leave the work to paddle everybody that comes along over the lake?"

"We have," said Lawry. "I must look out for the family now."

There was a good wind, and the boys returned to the ferry-house in the bateau. Before they had finished their breakfast, the ferry-horn sounded, and Lawry was obliged to take a team over to Pointville before the work could be resumed. Ethan was rather impatient under this delay; but he was too kind-hearted to make any unpleasant remark which would remind his friend of his father's crime.

CHAPTER IX
BEN WILFORD'S PLAN

While Lawry was ferrying the team over the lake, Ethan occupied himself in making a long-handled boat-hook, which might be useful in the operation of raising the steamer. While he was thus engaged, a young man, about eighteen years of age, coarsely dressed, and with a very red face, came down the road and stopped at the place where he was at work.

"What you making?" asked the young man.

"A boat-hook," replied Ethan.

"Do you belong here?" continued the stranger nodding his head toward the ferry-house.

"No; I'm only helping Lawry Wilford for a few days."

"The old man's got into hot water, they say."

"Yes."

"Well, he was always preaching to me about doing the right thing; and now he's fallen off the horse-block himself," added the young man, with a slight chuckle.

"It's bad for Mr. Wilford and his family."

"That's so. Where's Lawry now?"

"He has gone over with the ferry-boat."

"I reckon Lawry has to run the machine now."

"He has to run the ferry-boat."

"Well, he knows how. Lawry's smart--he is. I suppose you don't know me."

"I do not."

"I'm Lawry's brother; and that makes it that Lawry is my brother."

"Then you are Benjamin Wilford?"

"That's my name; but Ben Wilford sounds a good deal more natural to me. I heard the old man had got into trouble, and I came up to see about it, though I'm out of a job just now, and couldn't do anything better. I hear that Lawry owns a steamboat, and I didn't know but he'd want some help. Where is she?"

"She's on the bottom, out there by the Goblins," answered Ethan, pointing to the raft. "We are at work raising her."

"Can you get her up, do you think?"

"Yes; I have no doubt we shall have her at the top of the water by to-morrow night."

"I've come just in time, then," added the young man. "I think I know something about a steamboat."

Ethan did not like the looks of Lawry's brother. His bloated face was against him, and the young engineer, without knowing anything more about him than his swaggering manner and red face revealed, wished he had stayed away a few days longer.

"I'll go in and see the old woman, and get some breakfast; then I'll go up with you and see what you are doing," said Ben Wilford.

"We are going up as soon as Lawry comes back," answered Ethan, pointing to the ferry-boat.

The dissolute young man, who had just been discharged from his situation as a deck-hand on one of the steamers, for intemperance and neglect of duty, sauntered into the house; and the fresh breeze soon brought the impatient Lawry to the shore.

"Lawry, we have got some help," said Ethan.

"Who?"

"Your brother has just come."

"Ben?" asked the young lad, a troubled expression gathering on his face.

"Yes; he has gone into the house to get his breakfast."

"I'll go in and see him," added Lawry, who did not seem to be at all pleased with the news of his brother's arrival.

It is a sad thing for a brother to behave so badly that he cannot be welcome at his own home.

Mrs. Wilford shook hands with Benjamin as he entered. She was glad to see him, and her mother's heart went out toward him; but she was filled with doubts and fears. The young man only laughed while his mother wept at the story of the father's crime. He sat down to his breakfast, and declared that he had come home to take care of the family.

"I hope you are able to take care of yourself, Benjamin," replied his mother, as she glanced at his bloated face.

"I always did that, mother. The old man and I couldn't agree very well, but I reckon you and I can get along together. Lawry, how are you?" continued the returned wanderer, as his brother entered the room.

"Very well; how are you, Ben?" answered Lawry, as he shook hands with his brother.

"First-rate. How about the steamboat, Lawry?"

"She's all right; or, she will be, when we get her up."

"Do you think you can raise her?"

"I know we can."

"Well, I heard all about her up in the village, and I have come home to help you. I know all about steamboats, you know."

"What did you leave your place for?"

"The captain and I couldn't agree. I'm going to run an opposition line."

"Are you?"

"I am; bet your life I am."

"Where will you get your boats?"

"Don't want but one; and they say your boat is the finest little craft that ever floated on the lake."

"She is, without a doubt."

"Well, we can take some money out of the captain's pocket, at any rate. We'll make a fortune out of your boat, Lawry, if we get her up."

"I shall get her up by tomorrow night."

"I'll help you, Lawry."

"We don't need any help at present. I must go now, for Ethan is waiting for me."

"Who's Ethan?"

"Ethan French; he is the engineer of the steamer," answered the young pilot, moving toward the door.

"Hold on a minute, Lawry, and I'll be ready to go with you. I can show you how to do the business."

"I know now."

"You're smart, Lawry; but you're not so old as I am."

"I'm old enough to do this job."

"You haven't seen so much of steamboats as I have."

"Now, Benjamin, you mustn't interfere with Lawry's work," interposed Mrs. Wilford. "He knows what he is about."

"I'm not going to interfere with him; I'm only going to help him."

"If you really want to help me, I'll tell you what you can do," said Lawry.

"What's that?"

"You can run the ferry."

"Run the ferry!" exclaimed Ben. "Why, I know more about steamboats than you and your engineer put together. Do you suppose I'm going to run a ferry-boat when there's a job of this sort on hand?"

"You can help more in this way than in any other," persisted Lawry.

"Run a ferry-boat!" sneered Ben; "that isn't my style."

"We don't need any help on the steamer."

"Yes, you do. At any rate, I'll go down and see what you are about."

"What's that rock for?" he demanded, pointing to the sinker which lay on the skids.

"To sink the casks with," replied Ethan; and he explained the process by which the hogsheads were attached to the hull of the *Woodville*.

"Well, Lawry, if you had been studying seven years to get up the stupidest thing that could be thought of, you could not have got up a more ridiculous idea than this," said Ben, laughing contemptuously.

"How would you raise her?" asked Lawry quietly.

"Well, I wouldn't do it in this way, I can tell you. If you want me to take this job in hand for you, I'll do it. You might as well try to raise the Goblins as the steamer in this way."

"It is very easy to condemn the method," added Ethan indignantly; "but it isn't so easy to find a better one."

"You say you don't want any help from me," said Ben.

"If you can tell me any better way, I should like to hear it," replied Lawry.

"If you want me to raise your steamer, say the word."

"Let me know how you intend to do it, first," persisted Lawry. "It's easier to talk than it is to do."

"You're smart, Lawry; but you can't raise that steamer with those casks in seven years."

"I'll have her on the top of the water by to-morrow night," said the young pilot.

"No, you won't."

"You see! But we must go to work, Ethan."

"That's just my idea," said the engineer.

"Then you don't want me to do the job?" added Ben.

"No, I think not," replied Lawry, rather coldly.

"I think my way is the best."

"Perhaps it is; but I don't know what your way is."

"I'll tell you, Lawry, for I don't like to have you waste your time and strength doing nothing; besides, we want the steamer as soon as we can get her, or the season will be over."

"What do you mean by we, Ben?" asked Lawry quietly.

"Why, you and me, of course. I know something about steamers, and perhaps I should be willing to go captain of your boat, if you ever get her into working order."

"Perhaps you would," answered Lawry.

"Of course you mean to use the boat for the benefit of the family, now the old man is jugged and can't do anything more for them."

"To be sure I do."

"I'm willing to do my part. You can be the pilot, and the other fellow can be the engineer."

"And we can both of us have the privilege of obeying your orders," laughed Lawry.

"Well, I shouldn't be likely to interfere with you; your place would be in the wheel-house."

"And yours in the cabin, Captain Wilford. I can't stop to talk about this now. There comes Ethan with the cask."

"You might as well stop this foolish work first as last," sneered the would-be captain of the *Woodville*. "I was going to tell you how to raise her."

"Go on; we'll hear you, and work at the same time," said Ethan.

"I should get two of those canal-boats, having about eight feet depth of hold," continued Ben.

"Where would you get them?" demanded Lawry.

"Get them? Hire them, of course. You can get plenty of them at Port Henry."

"Have you any money in your pocket?"

"They wouldn't cost more than a hundred dollars."

"I haven't got even fifty dollars," said Lawry.

"They would trust you on the security of your steamer."

"I don't want to be trusted for any such purpose. What would you do with your canal-boats when you had got them?" asked Lawry.

"I would moor one on each side of the steamer, put a couple of timbers across them, pass a chain under the bow and stern of the sunken hull, and make fast to the timbers. Then I would let the water into the canal-boats, and sink them down to the rails. When I got them down as deep as I could, I would tighten the chains, till they bore taut on the timbers. Do you understand it, Lawry?"

"Certainly; I know all about the plan," replied the young pilot, with a smile.

"I don't believe you do," said Ben incredulously. "What would you do next?"

"Pump the water out of the two canal-boats, which would take about two days' time."

"You could rig extra pumps."

"Three of us, with three pumps, couldn't pump them out in two days."

"Well, the job is done when you have pumped them out."

"When you get the water out of the boats, you will have raised the steamer but three or four feet at most."

"Six feet, at least, for the canal-boats will come up where they were before."

"No; they won't; the weight of the steamer will press them down two or three feet."

An excited discussion followed upon this question; but Lawry and Ethan carried their point. It was plain that the buoyant powers of the two boats, as the water was pumped but of them, would raise the steamer three or four feet, leaving her suspended half-way between the surface and the bottom of the lake. Lawry wanted the aspirant for the captaincy of the **Woodville** to tell him what he would do next, for she could not be repaired while she was under water; but Ben was "nonplussed" and unable to answer.

"I can finish that job for you," said Lawry.

"She could be moored on the ways, and then hauled up."

"Perhaps she might, but I should rather put her on the ways from the top of the water. When I got her three feet from the bottom, I should move her toward the shore till she grounded."

"What then?" asked Ben.

"I should sink the canal-boats again, pump them out once more, and thus raise her three feet more; but it would take about three days every time we lifted her three feet. Ben, I think we could get her to the top of the water in about a fortnight by your plan. By mine, I shall have her up by to-morrow night."

"I'll bet you won't; or in a month, either. You know too much, Lawry," said Ben.

"I don't bet; but you shall see her at the ferry-landing by seven to-morrow evening if you are there."

The older brother, finding himself only a cipher on the raft, had consented to run the ferry in the afternoon, when the horn sounded; and the pilot and engineer were thus enabled to continue their labor without interruption.

CHAPTER X
HARD AT WORK

When Lawry and Ethan returned to the Goblins in the afternoon, they were delighted to find that the casks, all of which had been placed under the guards abaft the wheel, had actually produced an effect upon the steamer. The smokestack stood up more perpendicularly, indicating that the stern had been lifted from the bottom. Ethan was sure that the casks would bring the **Woodville** to the surface; but a very serious difficulty now presented itself.

About two-thirds of the length of the steamer's keel rested on a flat rock, whose surface was inclined downward toward the body of the lake, leaving the third next to the stern unsupported, under which the ropes had been easily drawn to retain the casks in their places. Of course it was impossible to draw any lines under the forward part of the keel, which rested on the flat rock, and it was necessary to devise some means for securing the casks to this portion of the hull.

"I have it," said Lawry.

"What is it?"

"We must sink more casks under the stern."

"But that will bring one end up, and leave the other on the rock."

"That isn't what I mean. If we put, say, two more hogsheads under the stern, they will raise it so we can get the ropes under the forward part of the hull."

"I understand; you are right, Lawry," replied Ethan.

When they returned to the ferry-house, they found Mr. Sherwood and the ladies there, who had come down to ascertain what progress had been made in the work. Ben Wilford had freely expressed his opinion that the enterprise would end in failure.

"Those boys know too much; that's all the trouble," said Ben.

"I was in hopes they would succeed in their undertaking," added Mr. Sherwood.

"So was I, sir; but there's no chance of their doing anything. I know something about steamboats, for I've been at work on them for three years."

"And you are quite sure they will fail?" asked Mr. Sherwood.

"Just as sure as I am of anything in this world. I told them what the trouble would be; but they know so much they won't hear me. I told them how it ought to be done."

"Here they come; they can speak for themselves," said Mr. Sherwood. "How do you get along, Lawry?"

"First-rate, sir."

"Indeed! Your brother thinks you are going to make a failure of the job."

"Perhaps we are, sir; but we don't believe it yet--do we, Ethan?"

"We don't."

"Lawry, wouldn't you be willing to sell out your interest in the *Woodville* at a small figure?" laughed Mr. Sherwood.

"No, sir!"

"Your brother, who seems to be a person of some experience in such matters, thinks you will not be able to raise the steamer. If that is likely to be the case, I don't want you to waste your time and strength for nothing. I should be glad to employ some men to raise the *Woodville* for you."

"Thank you, sir. You are very kind," replied Lawry.

"If you like, we will ride down to Port Henry to-night, and employ a man to do the job."

"I think we shall succeed, sir."

"What's the use of talking, Lawry?" interposed Ben. "You'll not get her up in seven years."

"Don't you think you had better give it up, Lawry?" asked Mr. Sherwood.

"Not yet, sir."

"What do you think, Lawry? Hadn't you better let me employ a man to do the work?"

"Ethan and I can do it very well, sir."

"Perhaps you can; but we wish to have the steamer in working order as soon as possible, and we may hasten the joy by employing men of experience to do it."

"Haste and waste," said Lawry, laughing. "Mr. Sherwood, I am satisfied we can raise the *Woodville*. We don't want any help. If we don't get her up by to-morrow night, I will let some one else take hold; but it will cost a heap of money."

"It shall not cost you anything, Lawry. I haven't half paid the debt of gratitude I owe you."

"Oh, never mind that, sir! I only want one more day."

"You are very confident, my boy, and I hope you will succeed," added Mr. Sherwood, as he turned to depart.

"Take him up, Lawry," said Ben. "Let him raise her. He will do it at his own expense, and perhaps he will give me the job."

"Not to-night."

"You are a fool, Lawry!" exclaimed Ben.

"Perhaps I am. Time will tell."

"He offered to pay for raising her, and you wouldn't let him do it!"

"He has made me a present of the steamer as she lies; and I don't ask anything more of him."

"Take all you can get, Lawry. That's the only way to get along in this world."

Ethan slept with his fellow workman at the cottage that night, and at daylight in the morning they were on their way to the Goblins. At breakfast-time two casks had been sunk under the bow of the steamer, for they had become so familiar with the work that it was carried on with greater rapidity than at the first.

At breakfast they were laughed at again by Ben Wilford; but they chose to keep still, made no replies, and gave no information in regard to the progress of the work. At the earnest request of Lawry, seconded by Mrs. Wilford, Ben consented to run the ferry that day, and the young engineers took their dinners with them when they went down to the Goblins. They were full of hope, and confidently expected to return to the landing at night with the *Woodville*.

At eleven o'clock four more hogsheads had been placed under the guards. The steamer swayed a little in the water; the stern had risen about two feet; and it was evident that she was on the point of floating. The boys were intensely excited at the bright prospect before them.

"Lawry, the work is nearly done," said Ethan.

"That's so; I think a couple of those barrels will finish it," answered the young pilot. "I see two anchors at her bow."

"Yes, there are two anchors and about forty fathoms of small chain- cable on board of her."

"I see them; and I think we had better fish them up."

"That's a good idea."

With the long boat-hook which Ethan had made, the cables were hauled up and coiled away on the raft, which had been placed over the bow of the sunken vessel. When the chains, which were bent onto the anchors, were hauled taut, the sinker rope, still in the block, and wound on the windlass of the derrick, was made fast to one of them, and the anchor drawn up. The operation was then repeated on the other anchor.

"Hurrah! hurrah!" shouted Lawry, as they began to turn the windlass. "She's coming up."

"Hurrah!" repeated Ethan, and the faces of both boys glowed with excited joy, as the sunken vessel followed the anchor up to the surface of the water.

It was necessary to move the raft, and the anchor was hauled out over the top of the bulwarks. The **Woodville** rose till her plank-sheer was even with the surface of the water. The boys shouted for joy; they were almost beside themselves with the excitement of that happy moment. They had conquered; success had crowned their labors.

"The job is done!" cried Lawry.

"That's so! Where is your brother now?" exclaimed Ethan.

"We have got her up sooner than I expected. I move you we have our dinner now."

"I don't feel much like dinner."

"I do."

"What is to be done next?"

"We must get her up a little farther out of the water. We can easily get some more casks under her now; but let us have some dinner first."

They sat down on a timber on the raft, and ate the dinner they had brought with them. They could not keep their eyes off the steamer during the meal, and they continued to discuss the means of completing the work they had begun.

After dinner the labor was renewed with redoubled energy. Four more casks were attached to the bow, and four removed from the stern; the effect of which was to lift the bow out of the water, while the deck at the after part was again submerged. This was Lawry's plan for ascertaining the extent of the injury which the hull had received. It now appeared that, when the **Woodville** struck the Goblins, she had slid upon a flat rock, while a sharp projection from the reef had stove a hole, not quite three feet in diameter, just above her keel.

"Now we must stop this hole," said Lawry; "and we may as well do it here as anywhere."

"That's just my idea," responded Ethan. "There's a painted floor-cloth in the kitchen, which will just cover it. I will get it."

"Have you any small nails on board?"

"Plenty of them."

The kitchen and the engineer's storeroom were now out of water, so that Ethan had no difficulty in procuring the articles needed in stopping up the hole. A couple of slats were placed over the aperture to prevent the floor-cloth from being forced in by the pressure of the water. Both of the boys then went to work nailing on the carpet, which was new and very heavy. The nails were put very close together, and most of them being carpet-tacks, with broad heads, they pressed the oilcloth closely down to the wood-work. It was not expected entirely to exclude the water; but the leakage could be easily controlled by the pumps.

Several of the casks were now removed from the bow to the stern, until the hull sat even on the water. All the heavy articles on deck, including the contents of the "chain-box," were transferred to the raft, and the laborers were ready to commence the long and trying operation of pumping her out. It was now six o'clock, and it was plain that this job could not be finished that night. The wind was beginning to freshen, and there were indications of bad Weather. Lawry had at first intended to move the **Woodville** up to the ferry-landing as soon as she floated; but Ethan, for certain reasons, which were satisfactory to his fellow laborer, wished to pump her out where she was; and it was found to be a very difficult thing to tow her up to the ferry in her water-logged condition.

It was not safe to leave her, with the prospect of a heavy blow, so near the Goblins, and they carried out the anchors in the wherry, and with the assistance of the capstan on the forward deck heaved her out into a secure position. The **Woodville** was safe for the night, and the supper-horn was sounding at the ferry-house. Nearly exhausted by their severe exertions, the boys returned to the cottage.

"I'm so glad that you have done it!" exclaimed Mrs. Wilford, when they went in to supper.

She had been a deeply interested observer of the operations of the young engineers, and her heart had bounded with emotions of joy, in unison with theirs, when she saw the steamer rise to the surface of the lake.

"I knew we should do it, mother," replied Lawry. "Where is Ben?"

"I don't know where he is. He went away just after dinner, and I haven't seen him since," added the mother.

"But I saw the ferry-boat go over in the middle of the afternoon."

"I know you did."

"But who went over with her?"

"I did," answered Mrs. Wilford quietly.

"You, mother?"

"Yes, Lawry; there was no one else to go, unless I called you, and I couldn't bear to take you away from your work. I've been over in the ferry times enough to know how to manage the boat."

"Ben said he would take care of the ferry."

"He doesn't always do as he promises," said Mrs. Wilford sadly.

Lawry thought it was very kind of his mother to run the ferry-boat, rather than disturb him at his work; but he did not like to have her do such labor. When he went out after supper, he found the wind was still quite fresh, and he was afraid that some accident might happen to the steamer in the night. If the casks got loose, she would sink again. While he and Ethan were talking about it, Ben Wilford returned home; and it was evident from his looks and actions that he had been drinking too much.

CHAPTER XI
ME. SHERWOOD AND PARTY

Well, Lawry, I don't see the steamer at the ferry-landing," said Ben Wilford. "You know, you promised to have her up here to-night; but I knew you wouldn't."

"We thought we wouldn't bring her up to-night," replied Lawry coldly.

"I knew you wouldn't, my boy. You didn't keep your promise."

"And you didn't keep yours."

"I didn't make any. If I'd promised to fetch that steamer up, she'd been here."

"You promised to run the ferry, and you left it."

"No, I didn't, Lawry. Don't you talk so to me. You know too much," added Ben angrily. "You never will raise that steamer in two thousand years."

"There she is," replied Lawry quietly, as he pointed in the direction of the Goblins.

Ben looked at her; he did not seem to be pleased to find her on the top of the water. His oft-repeated prophesy had been a failure, and Lawry was full as smart as people said he was.

"Humph!" said he. "She isn't much of a steamboat if those barrels brought her up."

"There she is; and I have done all I promised to do."

"What are you going to do next, Lawry?"

"I'm going to pump her out next."

"You'd better do it pretty quick, or she'll go to the bottom again," added Ben, as he walked into the house.

"There comes Mr. Sherwood, with the ladies," said Lawry, as he glanced up the road.

"I congratulate you, boys," said Mr. Sherwood, as he grasped Lawry's hand. "We gave three cheers for you on the hill, when we saw that you had raised the ***Woodville***."

"Thank you, sir. We worked pretty hard, but we were successful."

"You have done bravely," said Mrs. Sherwood. "We thought, from what your brother said last night, that you would fail."

"Ethan and I didn't think so."

"I suppose you wouldn't sell very cheap to-night, Lawry," added Mr. Sherwood.

"No, sir; the ***Woodville*** is a gift, and I should not be willing to sell her at any price."

"Well, Lawry, I am as glad as you are at your success. Do you want any help yet?"

"No, sir; we are just going on board of her to stay overnight, for we are afraid the heavy wind will do mischief."

"I wouldn't do that. You must rest to-night."

"I'm afraid something will happen if we don't look out for her."

"Are you going to pump her out to-night?"

"We may begin pretty early in the morning," said Lawry, with a smile.

"Haste and waste, my boy. If you stay on board of her to-night, and get sick, you will not make anything by your labor."

"If the wind goes down, we shall sleep ashore as usual. I don't think it blows quite so hard as it did."

"I don't," added Ethan.

"Boys, you mustn't overdo this thing," added Mr. Sherwood seriously.

His wife whispered to him just then.

"Yes, Bertha," he continued. "I'll tell you what I'm going to do, Lawry. I have four men at work for me. I can spare them one day, and they shall pump out the ***Woodville*** for you."

"You needn't object," interposed Mrs. Sherwood.

"Indeed you must not, Lawry," added Miss Fanny. "I am afraid you will both be sick if you work so hard."

"We can easily pump her out ourselves," said Ethan.

"You needn't say a word, Ethan," added Fanny Jane.

"I suppose we shall have to submit," replied Lawry, laughing. "We can't oppose the ladies."

"Just as you say, Lawry," said Ethan.

"You shall have the men to-morrow, boys. Now you must go to bed, and not think of the steamer till morning," continued Mr. Sherwood.

As the wind seemed to be subsiding, the boys went into the house; and though it was not quite dark, they "turned in," tired enough to sleep without rocking. Ben was at his supper, in no pleasant frame of mind. He was dissatisfied with himself, and with his brother, who had succeeded in his undertaking contrary to his prophecy. He was envious and jealous of Lawry. Now that his father was away, he thought he ought to be the chief person about the house, being the oldest boy.

"I'm not going to stay at home, and be a nobody," said he angrily.

"We don't wish you to be a nobody," replied his mother.

"Yes, you do; Lawry is everybody, and I'm nobody."

"You've been drinking, Benjamin."

"What if I have! I'm not going to stay here, and play second fiddle to a little boy."

"What are you talking about, Benjamin? Lawry has not interfered with you. He will treat you kindly and respectfully, as he treats everybody."

"He don't mind any more what I say than he does the grunting of the pigs."

"What do you want him to do?"

"I want him to pay some attention to what I say," snarled Ben. "I suppose he thinks that steamboat belongs to him."

"Certainly he does," replied Mrs. Wilford.

"I don't."

"Don't you? Whom does it belong to, then?"

"I'm not a fool, mother; I know a thing or two as well as some others. Lawry is not of age."

"Neither are you."

"I know that, but I'm older than he is."

"You are old enough to behave better."

"How do you expect me to be anybody here, when I have to knock under to my younger brother? I say the steamer don't belong to Lawry any more than she does to me. I have just as much right in her as he has."

"What do you mean by talking so, Benjamin? You know that Mr. Sherwood gave the steamer to Lawry, and the bill of sale is in Lawry's name."

"I don't care for that! she's just as much mine as she is his, and he'll find that out when she gets to running. Lawry's a minor, and can't hold any property; you know that just as well as I do."

"What if he is? I think he will be permitted to hold the steamboat, and run her."

"I don't think so. I was talking with Taylor, who holds the mortgage on this place, and he don't think so," added Ben, in a tone of triumph.

"What did he say?"

"Well, he means to attach the steamboat on the note he holds against father."

"He will not do that!" replied Mrs. Wilford.

"He says so, anyhow."

"He will foreclose the mortgage on the place if he wants to get his money."

"The place will not sell for enough to pay his note, and he knows it. No matter about him--the steamboat belongs to father, just as much as the ferry-boat does; and I think I ought to have something to say about her."

"If you want to do anything for the family, why can't you run the ferry-boat, Benjamin?"

"And let Lawry run the steamboat? Not if I know myself!" replied Ben, with savage emphasis. "He may run the ferry-boat, and I'll run the steamer."

"That would be neither fair nor right. The steamer belongs to Lawry, and I will never consent that he shall be turned out of her."

"I don't want to turn him out of her. I'll take charge of her, and he may go pilot; that's all he's good for."

"You mean that you'll be captain?"

"That's what I mean."

"I don't think Lawry will want any one to be captain over him.

"If I don't run that steamer, nobody shall!" said Ben angrily, as he rose and left the house.

"Good evening, Mrs. Wilford," said Mr. Sherwood. "Has Lawry gone to bed?"

"Yes, an hour ago."

"Is he asleep?"

"I suppose he is."

"All right, then."

"What in the world are you going to do with such a crowd of men, Mr. Sherwood?"

"I'm going to help the boys finish their job. Ethan told me they had stopped the leak, and it only remained to pump out the steamer. I am going to do this job; and I have men enough to finish it in a couple of hours."

"I should think you had," added Mrs. Wilford.

"I have gathered together all the men I could find. Don't say a word to the boys, if you please. I intend to surprise them. They will find the steamer free of water in the morning."

"You are very kind, Mr. Sherwood, to take so much trouble."

"The boys have worked so well that they deserve encouragement. May I take the ferry-boat to convey my men up to the steamer?"

"Certainly, sir."

Mr. Sherwood encouraged the men to work well by the promise of extra pay; and the laborers seemed to regard the occasion as a grand frolic. They exerted themselves to the utmost, and the buckets flew along the lines, while the pumps rolled out the water in a continuous flow. As the steamer, relieved of the weight that pressed her down, rose on the surface of the lake, it was only necessary to lift the water from below and pour it upon the deck, from which it would run off itself.

The job did not last long before such a strong force; and in two hours the work of the bailers was done. Ethan had fully described the method by which the hole in the hull of the *Woodville* had been stopped; but Mr. Sherwood had some doubts in regard to the strength of the material, and he went below to examine the place. Lawry and his fellow laborer had had no opportunity to test the strength and fitness of the work they had done, while the boat was full of water.

On examination, Mr. Sherwood found several small jets of water streaming through the seams between the planks, outside of the canvas carpet, which he stopped with packing from the engineer's storeroom. The braces which the boys had put over the hole kept the oilcloth in position, and when the packing had been driven into the open seams with a chisel and mallet, hardly any water came in around the aperture. The boys were warmly commended by their partial friend for the skill they had displayed in stopping the leak; and some of the men, who were familiar with vessels, that the steamer would not leak ten strokes an hour.

It was therefore safe to leave her; and Mr. Sherwood was satisfied that the boys would not find the water up to the bottom of the cabin floor in the morning. He carefully examined every part of the steamer to assure himself that everything was right before he left her. The pumps were tried again, just before they embarked for home, but they yielded only a few strokes of water.

The party returned to the landing, and Mr. Sherwood cautioned the men not to make any noise as they passed the cottage, fearful that the boys might be awakened and the delightful surprise in store for them spoiled. But Lawry and Ethan, worn out by the fatigue and excitement of the day, slept like logs, and the discharge of a battery of artillery under their chamber window would hardly have aroused them from their slumbers. The men went to their several homes, and all was quiet at the ferry.

CHAPTER XII
FROM DESPONDENCY TO REJOICING

Ben Wilford made his way to the deck of the steamer, and in the darkness stumbled against the cables, with which the boat was anchored. He was bent on mischief, and he unstoppered the cables, permitting them to run out and sink to the bottom of the lake. The wind was blowing, still pretty fresh, from the west, and the steamer, now loosened from her moorings, began to drift toward the middle of the lake.

"They'll find I'm not a nobody," whined he. "She'll go down in the deep water this time."

The drunken villain then stumbled about the deck till he found the lines which kept the hogsheads in place under the guards. Groaning, crying, and swearing, he untied and threw the ropes overboard. Some of the casks, relieved of the pressure on them by the removal of the water from the interior of the hull, came out from their places and floated off. Ben rolled into the wherry again, and with the boat-hook hauled the others out. Satisfied that he had done his work, and that the *Woodville* would soon go down in the middle of the lake, he pulled as rapidly as his intoxicated condition would permit toward the ferry-landing.

"They'll find I'm not a nobody," he repeated, as he rowed to the shore. "They can't raise her now; and they'll never see her again."

Intoxicated as he was, he had not lost his sense of caution. He knew that he had done a mean and wicked action, which it might be necessary for him to conceal. As he approached the landing, he wiped his eyes, and choked down the emotions that agitated him. He tried to make no noise, but his movements were very uncertain; he tumbled over the thwarts, and rattled the oars, so that, if those in the cottage had not slept like rocks, they must have heard him. He reeled up to the house, took off his shoes, and crept upstairs to his room. He made noise enough to wake his mother; but Lawry and Ethan were not disturbed.

The wretch had accomplished his work. He was satisfied, as he laid his boozy head upon the pillow, that the **Woodville** was even then at the bottom of the lake, with a hundred feet of water rolling over her. It was two o'clock in the morning; but the vile tipple he had drank, and the deed he had done, so excited him that he could not sleep. He tossed on his bed till the day dawned, and the blessed light streamed in at the window of the attic.

"Four o'clock!" shouted Lawry, as the timepiece in the kitchen struck the hour. "All hands ahoy, Ethan!"

His enthusiastic fellow laborer needed no second call, and leaped out of bed. Ben was still awake, and the lapse of the hours had in some measure sobered him.

"It's a fine day, Ethan," said Lawry.

"Glad of that. How long do you suppose it will take to pump her out?"

"All day, I think; but we are to have four men to help us. I was considering that matter when I went to sleep last night," replied Lawry. "I was thinking whether we could not rig a barrel under the derrick so as to get along a little faster than the pumps will do it.

"Perhaps we can; we will see."

"Where is your steamer?" asked Ben, rising in bed.

"We anchored her near the Goblins," replied Lawry.

"She isn't there now," added Ben.

"How do you know?" demanded the pilot.

"I've been sick, and couldn't sleep; so I got up and went outdoors. She isn't where you left her, and I couldn't see anything of her anywhere."

"Couldn't see her!" exclaimed Ethan.

"I knew very well she wouldn't stay on top of the water. Casks wouldn't keep her up," said Ben maliciously.

Lawry rushed out of the room to the other end of the house, the attic window of which commanded a full view of the lake. As his brother had declared, the **Woodville** was not at her anchorage where they had left her; neither was she to be seen, whichever way he looked.

"She is gone!" cried he, returning to his chamber.

"Of course she is gone," added Ben.

"I don't understand it."

"She has gone to the bottom, of course, where I told you she would go. You were a fool to leave her out there in the deep water. She has gone down where you will never see her again."

"It was impossible for her to sink with all those casks under her guards," said Ethan.

"I guess you will find she has sunk. I told you she would. If you had only minded what I told you, she would have been all right, Lawry."

Both of the boys seemed to be paralyzed at the discovery, and made no reply to Ben. They could not realize that all the hard labor they had performed was lost. It was hard and cruel, and each reproached himself because they had not passed the night on board of the steamer, as they had purposed to do.

"Well, it's no use to stand here like logs," said Lawry, "If she has sunk, we will find out where she is."

"I reckon you'll never see her again, Lawry. Those old casks leaked, I suppose, and when they were full of water the steamer went down again; or else they broke loose from her when the wind blew so hard."

"It didn't blow much when we went to bed. What time did you come home, Ben?"

"I don't know what time it was," he answered evasively.

"Come, Ethan, let's go and find out what the matter is," continued Lawry, as he led the way downstairs.

Mrs. Wilford was not up, but she was awake, and was anticipating with great satisfaction the pleasure of the surprise which awaited the boys, when they discovered that the steamer had been freed from water. They left the house, and went down to the ferry. The **Woodville** certainly was not where they had left her; not even the top of her smokestack could be seen peering above the water to inform them that she still existed.

"Well, Lawry, we may as well go out to the place where we left her. If she has sunk, we may be able to see her," said Ethan.

They got into the boat; but one of the oars was gone. Ben had lost it overboard when he landed, and it had floated off. There was another pair in the woodshed of the house, and Lawry went up for them. As he entered the shed, he met his mother, who had just risen, and gone out for wood to kindle the fire. The poor boy looked so sad and disconsolate that his long face attracted her attention.

"What's the matter, Lawry?" she asked.

"The steamer has sunk again," replied the son.

"Sunk again!" exclaimed his mother.

"She is not to be seen, and Ben says she has gone down."

"Ben says so?"

"Yes; he told us of it before we came down. We are going to look for her now," answered Lawry.

What Lawry had said excited the suspicion of his mother, as she thought of the malicious words of her older son on the preceding evening. She was excited and indignant; she feared he had executed the wicked purpose which she was confident he had cherished. She went into the house, and upstairs to the room where Ben still lay in bed.

"Benjamin, what have you done?" demanded she.

"I haven't done anything. I'm a nobody here!" replied the inebriated young man, with surly emphasis.

"What did you mean last night when you said that you should run that steamer, or nobody should?" asked Mrs. Wilford.

"I meant just what I said. You and Lawry both said I shouldn't run her--and she has gone to the bottom again; she'll stay there this time."

"Oh, Benjamin!" said his mother, bursting into tears. "How could you be so wicked?"

"Did you think I'd stay round here, and be a nobody?" growled the wretched young man.

"Did you sink that steamer?"

"What if I did?"

"Oh, Benjamin!"

"You needn't cry about it. Next time, you'd better not try to make a nobody out of me."

"Don't you think I've had trouble enough, without trying to make more for me?" sobbed the distressed mother.

"If you had told Lawry to give me the charge of the steamer, he would have done it," whined Ben.

"I shouldn't tell him any such thing!" replied Mrs. Wilford indignantly. "A pretty captain of a steamboat you would make! You are so tipsy now you can't hold your head up!"

"I'm as sober as you are."

Mrs. Wilford knew that it was useless to talk to a person in his condition, and she left him to sleep off the effect of his cups if he could, after the evil deed he had done. Full of sympathy for Lawry, under his great affliction, she left the house, and hastened down to the landing, to learn, if possible, the condition of the *Woodville*. Lawry and Ethan were in the wherry, returning to the shore, when she reached the landing.

"Hurrah! hurrah!" shouted both of the boys, in unison, as Mrs. Wilford came in sight.

"What now?" asked the anxious mother.

"She's safe, mother! She has not sunk," replied Lawry.

"Where is she? I don't see her anywhere," added Mrs. Wilford, scanning the lake in every direction.

"Over on the other side," replied Lawry.

"What's the reason she didn't sink?" continued his mother.

"The casks kept her up, of course. We want something for breakfast and for dinner, mother, for she is so far off we can't come home till we have pumped her out, and I won't leave her again till I am sure she's all right."

"What shall I do about the ferry, mother?" asked Lawry. "Will Ben run the boat to-day?"

"Don't trouble yourself about the ferry, Lawry. If Benjamin won't take care of it, I will."

"I don't want you to do it, mother."

"I think your brother will run the boat; at any rate, you needn't give it a thought."

Mrs. Wilford was quite as happy as the boys to find that the steamer was not at the bottom of the lake again; and she returned to the cottage with a light heart, when she had seen the wherry leave the shore.

From the deepest depths of despondency, if not despair, the young engineers had been raised to the highest pinnacle of hope and joy when the **Woodville** was discovered on the other side of the lake. She had drifted in behind a point of land, and could not be seen from the ferry. They had gone out to the place where she had been anchored, near the Goblins; and while they were gazing down into the deep water in search of her, Ethan happened to raise his eyes and saw her on the other side of the lake. What a thrill went through his heart as he recognized her! And what a thrill he communicated to Lawry when he pointed her out to him!

"Why, the casks are all gone!" exclaimed Ethan.

"All gone!" replied Lawry.

"She must be aground," added Ethan; "but she sets out of water a great deal farther than when we left her."

"We shall soon find out what the matter is," continued Lawry. "She is safe, and on the top of the water; that's enough for me at the present time."

"What does this mean?" he exclaimed.

"I don't know. The water couldn't have run out of her without some help," replied Ethan.

"I don't understand it," added Lawry. "The casks are all gone, and the steamer has been pumped out. Somebody must have done this work."

"That's true," said Ethan. "Somebody has certainly been here."

"There's no doubt of that; but I can't see, for the life of me, what they wanted to set her adrift for."

"Nor I; they were good friends to pump her out for us, whoever they were. In my opinion, Mr. Sherwood knows something about this job."

"But slipping the cables looks just as though they intended to have her smashed up on the shore," added Lawry. "The anchors are not here, and, of course, they are on the bottom of the lake. I don't see through this business."

"Nor I, either; but one thing we can see through; the steamer is safe, with the water all pumped out of her. We may as well go to work, and get her over to the ferry."

This was good counsel, and without losing any more time in attempts to fathom what was dark and strange, they commenced the labors of the day.

CHAPTER XIII
GETTING UP STEAM

A survey of the position of the **Woodville** showed that she was slightly aground at the stern; but Ethan was confident that a few turns of the wheels would bring her off. The boys then tried the pumps; but after less than a hundred strokes they refused to yield any more water. They then carefully examined every part of the interior below the decks.

"She's all right," said Lawry. "What shall we do now?"

"Get up steam," replied Ethan. "I have a couple of hours' work to do on the engine; but we will start the furnaces at once."

"Can't I make the fire?" asked Lawry.

"Yes, if you know how."

"You can show me. I don't know much about steam-boilers and engines."

"We will get our dry wood out of the wherry, and I will help you start the fire. While I am at work on the engine, you will have to overhaul your steering-gear, and see that it is all right. The chains and pulleys will need to be oiled."

Lawry got into the wherry, and threw the dry wood on deck. Ethan had not expected to kindle the fires till night, when he hoped the water would be below the furnaces. It was a grateful surprise to be able at once to go to work on the engine. He was enthusiastic in his fondness for machinery, and that of the **Woodville** was his particular pet.

After he had tried the valves on the boiler, and assured himself that it contained the proper supply of water, the fires were started in the furnaces. There was plenty of wood and coal on board, though the former was so wet that it would not burn without some assistance, which was furnished by the dry fuel brought off in the wherry. In a little while the furnaces were roaring with the blaze from the wood, and the coal was shoveled in. Ethan, having dried a quantity of the wet packing, commenced rubbing down and oiling the machinery. He was in his element now, and never was a young man in a higher state of keen enjoyment.

While he was thus engaged, Lawry overhauled the steering apparatus, rubbed down the wheel, oiled the pulleys, and satisfied himself that everything was in working order. The situation and the work were in the highest degree exhilarating. It was not labor to clean and adjust the gear; it was a pleasure such as he had never realized from the most exciting sports. He could hardly repress the rapture he felt when he saw the black smoke from the pine wood pouring out of the smokestack.

"This is my steamer," said he to himself. "I am the owner of her."

The thought made him laugh with joy. He stood up at the wheel, and though he could not turn it, because the rudder was fast in the sand, he knew exactly how he should feel when he stood in this position with the **Woodville** gliding swiftly over the bright waters of the lake.

The steering-gear was in perfect order, so far as he could judge without using it, and Ethan was still busy at the engine. Lawry could not deny himself the pleasure of a survey of the steamer, for the purpose of admiring her comforts and conveniences. He walked up and down the main-deck, entered the saloon and the cabin, visited the forehold, and opened the doors of the various apartments forward of the paddle-boxes. It is true, everything was in a state of "confusion worse confounded." Carpets were soaked with water, curtains were drabbled and stained, sofas and chairs upset in the cabin and saloon; while in the kitchen and storerooms, shelves and lockers had been emptied, and their contents strewed in wild disorder about the apartments.

But Lawry knew how order could be brought out of chaos, and the derangement of furniture and utensils did not disturb him. It would be a delightful occupation to restore harmony to these shelves and lockers, to bring order and neatness out of the confusion which reigned in every part of the steamer. When he had completed his survey, he went to the engine-room, and offered his services to Ethan for duty in his department. As the engineer had nothing for him to do, he returned to the kitchen, and busied himself in putting things to rights there, foreseeing that this apartment would soon be needed. He made a fire in the galley, in order to dry the room more speedily, and then occupied his time in picking up the tins and the kettles, and putting them in their places.

While he was examining the lockers and shelves, he found part of a leg of bacon, and some potatoes, which had been left from the stores used by the crew on the passage from New York up to the lake. There were coffee and tea in the canisters, sugar in the buckets, butter and salt in the boxes; though all these articles had been more or less soaked in the water, depending upon the tightness of the vessels that held them. There was a good fire in the stove, and a bright thought entered Lawry's excited brain; he and his companion would breakfast on fried ham and potatoes, flanked with hot coffee!

Lawry was a cook of no mean accomplishments, and he immediately went to work in carrying out his brilliant idea. Somehow, it is a singular fact that boys have a special delight in "getting up something to eat" in the woods, on the water, and generally in all out-of-the-way places. A dinner at Parker's or Delmonico's is not to be compared with baked potatoes and roasted ears of corn in the woods, or with fried fish and potatoes in a boat or on an island. The young pilot was no exception to the common rule, and in a state of rapture known only to the amateur cook of tender years, he put on the teakettle, pared and sliced the potatoes, and put a quantity of the brown mud from the canister into the coffeepot.

Things were hissing and sizzling on the stove in the most satisfactory manner, and Lawry presided over the frying-pan with a grace and dignity which would have been edifying in a professional cook. While the ham was cooking, he wiped the dishes with a cloth he had dried at the fire, and set the table on the broad bench at the end of the kitchen. The meat and the potatoes were "done to a turn," but the coffee had a suspicious look, owing to the absence of the fish-skin, or other ingredient, for settling it. The contents of the basket brought from home were tastily disposed in dishes on the table, and breakfast was ready. We will venture to say that, in spite of the disadvantages under which this meal was prepared, many steamboat men have sat down to a less satisfactory banquet.

Lawry, chuckling with delight at what he had done, rang the hand-bell he found in the kitchen, at the door. If Ethan had smelled the savory viands in the course of preparation for him, he had made no sign; but he was probably too busy to heed anything but the darling engine he was so affectionately caressing with handfuls of packing and spurts of oil.

"What's that bell for, Lawry?" shouted he.

"Breakfast's ready," replied Lawry.

"I wouldn't stop to eat now--would you?"

"Things will be cold if you don't."

"Cold?" laughed Ethan.

"Yes--cold. What's the use of having a kitchen if you don't use it?"

"You're a good one!" shouted Ethan. "Why didn't you tell me what you were about?"

"I didn't want to spoil your appetite."

"You are a first-rate fellow, Lawry. Your breakfast looks tip-top, and I shall do full justice to it; but I must go and look at the boiler and the fires before I eat."

They sat down to breakfast when Ethan had returned and washed the smut from his face and hands. Lawry poured out the coffee, and helped his companion to ham and potatoes. The engineer ate with good relish.

"Your ham and potatoes are first-rate, Lawry; but I've seen better coffee than this," said he.

"I had nothing to settle it, and there is no milk on board."

"We had some fish-skin, and there is plenty of condensed milk on board," replied Ethan.

The coffee was subjected to a new process, and the condensed milk prepared for use. By the time the substantials of the feast had been discussed, some pretty good coffee was ready for them. The boys ate their breakfast with a zest they had never known before.

"Ethan!" exclaimed Lawry.

"What, Lawry?"

"Hold me down!" shouted the proprietor of the *Woodville*.

"What's the matter?"

"Hold me down! I shall go up if you don't. I can't hold in any longer. I'm so tickled, I feel as though I should fly away."

"Don't do it," laughed Ethan. "But I must go and look after the engine, or we may both go up, in a way that won't suit us;" and Ethan hurried down into the fire-room.

After taking a turn up and down the deck, Lawry curbed down his superfluous enthusiasm, and returned to the kitchen, where he extinguished the fire in the galley, and put away the dishes and kettles which had been used in getting breakfast. By this time Ethan had finished his work on the engine, and the steam gage indicated a sufficient pressure to work the machinery.

"All ready, Lawry!" shouted he.

"Is everything all right?"

"Yes, as good as new. Now, if you will go into the wheel-house, we will see what she will do."

"Hurrah!" shouted Lawry.

He pulled the bell for starting her, and with a thrill of delight he heard the wheels splashing in the water; and the great splurges began to roll up on the shore.

"Does she move?" asked Ethan, through the speaking-tube which communicated with the engine-room.

"No, she sticks fast," replied Lawry. "Give her a little more of it."

The wheels of the steamer turned rapidly for a moment, and the *Woodville* slid off the ground into deep water.

"Hurrah!" shouted Lawry, as he rang the bell to stop her. "She's all right now," he added, through the tube.

"Go ahead, then," replied the engineer.

"As soon as I make fast the wherry astern."

Before he went to the wheel-house he sounded the pumps again, and visited the forehold to examine the oilcloth over the aperture in the bow. There was but little water in the well, and the canvas carpet was faithful to its duty. There was nothing to fear, though Lawry couldn't help fearing.

"Are you all ready, Ethan?" called the pilot through the tube.

"All ready; but don't you think we had better hoist the flags, and go over in good style?" responded the engineer.

"Aye, aye."

The small American flag and the union jack, which had been taken from the poles the night before, and deposited in the locker of the wherry, were displayed, and Lawry returned to his post.

The pilot rang his bell to start, and the wheels turned slowly as Ethan opened the valve. The *Woodville* moved off from the shore, and Lawry's heart bounded as though it had been part of the engine. He grasped the spokes, and heaved the wheel over; the beautiful craft obeyed her helm.

"Hurrah! hurrah! hurrah!" shouted Lawry, at the mouth of the speaking-tube.

"Hurrah! hurrah! hurrah!" echoed back from the engine-room.

Lawry stood at the wheel, looking through the open window in front of him. It was his hour of triumph. As he gazed at the shore, he saw the ferry-boat start out from the landing. There was no vehicle in her, and as the steamer approached nearer to her, he saw that Mr. Sherwood and the ladies were on board of her. They were coming out to welcome and congratulate Ethan and himself upon the triumphant success of the enterprise. Mrs. Wilford was with them, and Ben held the steering oar.

Lawry informed his friend, through the tube, of the approach of the party. The ladies in the ferry-boat were waving their handkerchiefs, and Mr. Sherwood was swinging his hat.

"Whistle, Lawry!" shouted the engineer, as the pilot informed him what was taking place.

"Hurrah!" shouted the pilot, as he pulled the string.

As the **Woodville** came up to the bateau, Lawry rang to stop, and, swinging his hat out the window, gave three cheers all alone, while the ladies waved their handkerchiefs in reply.

CHAPTER XIV
CAPTAIN LAWRY

The bateau ran up to the steamer, and Ben made her fast at the forward gangway. Mr. Sherwood still cheered, and the ladies continued to wave their handkerchiefs.

"Won't you come on board?" said Lawry to the party.

"I shall, for one," replied Mr. Sherwood.

"I'm afraid of her," added Miss Fanny.

"There is nothing to fear, ladies. She is safe, and we are running her very slowly," continued the young pilot.

"Lawry knows where the rocks are," said Mrs. Wilford, "and I'll warrant you there is no danger."

With some misgivings, the ladies, who had suffered by the catastrophe when the **Woodville** was wrecked, permitted themselves to be handed to the deck of the steamer.

"I congratulate you on your success, Lawry," said Mr. Sherwood, as he stepped on board after the ladies. "You have worked bravely, and succeeded nobly;" and he grasped the hand of the pilot.

"Thank you, sir. I knew I could raise her, if I had fair play. I don't know but you are sick of your bargain, sir, in giving her to me."

"By no means, Captain Lawry," replied the rich man, laughing. "If the ladies succeed in overcoming their terror of steamboats, I suppose I can charter the boat for our party when we wish to use her."

"She's at your service always, sir," replied Lawry.

"Oh, I shall take her on the same terms that others do. When I use her, I shall pay you."

"That wouldn't be fair, sir. I couldn't take any money from you for the use of her," added Lawry, blushing.

"We will not talk about that now. When she is in condition for use, we will consider these questions. How did you find her this morning?" asked Mr. Sherwood, with a mischievous twinkle in his eye.

"We found the water all pumped out of her; and we didn't know what to make of it," answered Lawry.

All the visitors burst out laughing, and heartily enjoyed the astonishment and confusion of the young pilot.

"I don't understand it," exclaimed Lawry.

"The fairies, knowing what a good boy you are, Lawry, must have pumped her out for you," said Miss Fanny.

"Perhaps they did."

Mr. Sherwood then explained what he had done the preceding night, and the reason why he had done it. Ben Wilford, after fastening the ferry-boat at the stern of the steamer, had come on deck, and listened to the explanation. He saw in what manner his malice had been defeated, and he looked very much dissatisfied with himself and everybody on board.

"You were very kind, Mr. Sherwood, to take so much trouble upon yourself," said Lawry.

"It was no trouble at all; it was a great pleasure to me. But I don't understand how the steamer happened to be on the other side of the lake."

"I supposed the persons who bailed her out set her adrift. The casks were all knocked out from under the guards, and they are scattered all along the shore."

"Before my men left her last night, I went all over the boat to satisfy myself that everything was right. I examined the cables very carefully, and I am sure they were well stoppered at twelve o'clock, when we went on shore."

"I fastened the cable myself, and I don't think she could have broken loose herself."

Ben Wilford listened in sullen silence to this conversation, and his mother could hardly keep from crying as she thought of the guilt of her oldest son. She was not willing to tell Lawry what his brother had done, fearful that his indignation would produce a quarrel where brotherly love should prevail. She believed that Ben had attempted, while under the influence of liquor, to sink the **Woodville**, and that he would not do such a thing in his sober senses.

Neither Lawry nor Mr. Sherwood could explain in what manner the steamer had broken from her moorings and the oil-casks been removed from their fastenings; so they were obliged to drop the matter, congratulating themselves upon the present safety of the boat.

"We will go ashore with you, Captain Lawry, when you are ready," said Mr. Sherwood, after the question had been disposed of in this unsatisfactory manner.

"Captain Lawry!" sneered Ben.

"Certainly; he is the captain of the steamer--isn't he?" laughed Mr. Sherwood.

"It sounds big for a boy," growled Ben.

"He will make a good captain."

Ben turned and walked away, disgusted with the idea.

"I'm ready, sir," said Lawry.

"Where are you bound next, Captain Lawry?" asked Mr. Sherwood.

"I'm going to fish up the anchors we lost, and then to pick up the oil-casks," replied Lawry.

"Where do you intend to keep your steamer?"

"I hadn't thought of that, sir."

"You will need a wharf."

"We need one; but I think we shall have to get along without one."

"Where would be a good place to have one?"

"The deepest water is just below the ferry-landing. We could get depth enough for this boat by running a pier out about forty feet. Ethan and I can build some kind of a wharf, when we have time."

Mr. Sherwood said no more about the matter, and Ben landed the visitors in the ferry-boat. The **Woodville** then ran down to the Goblins, and towed the raft out to the spot where the anchors lay. A boat grapnel was dragged over the spot, the cables hooked, and the anchors hauled up with the derrick on the raft, from which they were transferred to the steamer.

Having obtained these necessary appendages of the steamer, they returned to the landing for the ferry-boat, in which they intended to load the oil-casks, and convey them to Pointville. Ben was at the landing when she arrived, and without any invitation, stepped on board the ferry-boat, and thence to the steamer.

"Don't you want some help, Lawry?" asked Ben.

"Yes; we should be glad of all the help we can get," replied Lawry pleasantly.

"Well, I'll help you."

"We have a good deal of hard work to do to-day," added the pilot. "I would like to get the boat on the ways at Port Henry to-night."

"That can be done easy enough."

Ben Wilford seemed now to have adopted a conciliatory policy, but it was evidently done for a purpose. When the *Woodville* reached the Goblins, he worked with good will in loading the ferry-boat, which was towed over to Pointville, and her cargo discharged. The casks, which had drifted over to the eastern shore of the lake, were then picked up, and landed at the same place. The man who had carted them down to the shore was engaged to convey them back to the barn of the oil speculator. It was noon by the time this work was all accomplished; and the *Woodville* again crossed the lake, and came to anchor in the deep water above the ferry-landing, as close to the shore as it was prudent for her to lie. Ethan banked his fires, and the boys went on shore to dinner, one at a time; for after the experience of the preceding night they would not leave the steamer alone for a single moment.

After dinner, Mr. Sherwood, who appeared to be as much interested in the little steamer as though she had not changed her ownership, came on board again, accompanied by the ladies. It had before been decided that the carpets should be taken up, the muslin curtains removed, and such portions of the furniture and utensils as had been injured by the water should be conveyed on shore to be cleaned, and put in proper order for use. In this labor Mr. Sherwood's party and Mrs. Wilford assisted, and by the middle of the afternoon everything had been removed. Ben Wilford aided very zealously, and his mother hopefully concluded that he was sorry for what he intended to do, and wished to remove any suspicion of evil intentions on his part.

The *Woodville* was now going down to Port Henry, where the repairs on her hull were to be made, and the pilot and engineer were to remain on board. Ben promised faithfully to run the ferry during Lawry's absence; and, cheered by the party on the shore, the *Woodville* departed for her destination. She ran at half speed, but reached the port before sunset. The next morning she went on the ways, and her repairs commenced. During that time Ethan was constantly employed on the engine, and when the steamer was restored to her native element there was not a suspicion of rust on the machinery.

Lawry was also as busy as a bee all the time, scrubbing the floors, cleaning the paint, and polishing the brass-work. When the boat was ready to return to Port Rock, she was in condition to receive her furniture. She was launched early in the morning, and Ethan proceeded at once to get up steam. Both of the boys were in the highest state of expectancy and delight; and when Lawry struck the bell to start her, he was hardly less excited than when he had done so for the first time after the water had been pumped out of her. All the bunting was displayed at the bow and stern, and the **Woodville** now plowed the lake at full speed. Her happy owner realized that she was good for ten miles an hour, which, for so diminutive a craft, was more than he had a right to expect.

"Hello!" shouted Lawry to himself, as the steamer approached the ferry-landing; "what's that?"

In the deep water which the young pilot had indicated as the best place for a wharf, a pier was in process of erection. A score of bridge-builders were sawing, hammering, and chopping, and Mr. Sherwood stood in their midst, watching their operations. The structure was not complete, but the mooring posts were set up, so that the **Woodville** could be made fast to them. Mr. Sherwood and the workmen gave three cheers as the steamer approached.

"Run her up here, Lawry!" shouted his wealthy friend. "Aye, aye, sir."

"You have taken this job out of my hands, sir," said Lawry, as he glanced at the wharf.

"Yes; I thought I could do it better than you could, as your time will be fully occupied."

"I think I should have found time enough to do what I intended; but of course I couldn't have built any such wharf as this."

"It is none too good."

"But I ought to pay for it out of the money I may earn with the boat."

"Never mind that, Lawry," added Mr. Sherwood.

The young captain explained what had been done during his absence, and informed his interested friend that the steamer was in condition to receive her furniture.

"Shall you have her ready for a trip by to-morrow?" asked Mr. Sherwood.

"Yes, sir."

"Because I have taken the liberty to engage her, in your name, for several parties."

"You are very kind, sir," replied Lawry.

"Have you fixed upon any price for her?"

"Ethan and I were talking over the matter. We shall need some help on board, and that will cost money. Coal is pretty high up here on the lake."

"Well, how much did you intend to charge for her by the day, or the hour?"

"We thought about three dollars an hour," replied Lawry, with much diffidence.

"Three dollars an hour! You are too modest by half," laughed Mr. Sherwood. "Make it five, at least. I told the parties I engaged for you that the price would not be less than fifty dollars a day."

"I'm afraid I shall make money too fast at that rate," added Lawry.

"No, you won't. It will cost a great deal of money to run the boat. What do you pay your engineer?"

"I don't know, sir; we have made no bargain yet."

"If Ethan does a man's work, you must pay him a man's wages. I suppose he wants to make his fortune."

"What do you think he ought to have?" asked Lawry.

"Three dollars a day," replied Mr. Sherwood promptly. "I dare say Ethan would not charge you half so much; but that is about the wages of a man for running an engine in these times."

"I am satisfied, if that is fair wages; though it is a great deal more than I ever made."

"Engineers get high wages. Then you want a fireman."

"I can get a boy, who will answer very well for a fireman."

"I think not, Lawry. You need a man of experience and judgment. He can save his wages for you in coal. The man whom I employed as a fireman is just the person, and he is at the village now."

"What must I pay him, sir?"

"Two dollars a day. Then your parties will want some dinner on board, and you will need a cook, and two stewards. A woman to do the cooking, and two girls to tend the table, will answer your purpose. You can obtain the three for about seven dollars a week; but your passengers must pay extra for their meals, and you need not charge the expenses of the steward's department to the boat."

"If you expect to succeed, Lawry, you must do your work well. Your boat must be safe and comfortable, and your dinners nice and well served. You will want two deck-hands. Your expenses, including coal, oil for machinery, and hands, will be about twenty dollars a day. If you add repairs, of which steamboats are continually in need, you will run it up to twenty-five dollars a day."

"That will leave me a profit of twenty-five dollars a day," added Lawry, delighted at the thought.

"If you are employed every day, it will; but you cannot expect to do anything with parties for more than two months in the year."

"I can get some towing to do; and I may make something with passengers."

"Parties will pay best in July and August, and perhaps part of September; but you must be wide-awake."

"I intend to be."

"I advise you to get up a handbill of your steamer, announcing that she is to be let to parties by the day, at all the large ports on the lake. There are plenty of wealthy people, spending the summer in this vicinity, who would be glad to engage her, even for a week at once."

"Will you write me a handbill, Mr. Sherwood?"

"Yes, and get it printed."

"Thank you, sir."

"The *Woodville* is engaged to me for to-morrow," added Mr. Sherwood.

CHAPTER XV
THE NEW CAPTAIN

Lawry was bewildered by the magnificence of the arrangements suggested by Mr. Sherwood; but if the **Woodville** was to be employed in taking out parties of genteel people, nothing less magnificent would answer the purpose. His influential friend, it appeared, had already exerted himself to procure employment of this kind for the steamer, and the proprietor of the beautiful craft was not only willing to conform to his ideas, but was grateful for the kindly interest he manifested in the prosperity of the enterprise.

Mrs. Wilford had engaged a cook, and two girls for the steward's department; the fireman was sent for; and two boys were employed as deck-hands.

Now, Lawry thought it was quite necessary that his crew should be trained a little before any passengers were received on board, and after Mr. Sherwood and his party had gone home, the fires were revived, and a short trip down the lake determined upon. As soon as there was steam enough for the purpose, the pilot, now the captain, rang his bell to back her, and the deck-hands were instructed in getting the fasts on board. Ben Wilford, who was standing on the wharf, cast off the hawsers, and then jumped aboard, himself. The bells jingled for a few moments, and then the **Woodville** went off on her course.

"This is all very fine," said Ben.

"First-rate," laughed Lawry.

"What am I to do?" demanded Ben, rather gruffly.

"You?" said the pilot.

"Everybody seems to have something to do with her except me."

"What do you want to do?"

"I suppose you think I'm not fit for anything."

"I had an idea that you would stay at home, and run the ferry-boat."

"Did you?" sneered Ben.

"Some one must do that; and of course I can't now."

"Hang the ferry-boat!"

"It must be run, or we shall forfeit the privilege."

"I shall not run it, whatever happens."

"I don't see how I can."

"Lawry, I don't think you are using me right," added Ben sourly.

"Why, what have I done?"

"You've got this boat, and though you know I'm a steamboat man, you don't say a word to me about taking any position on board of her."

"I don't know what position there is on board for you, unless you take a deck-hand's place."

"A deck-hand!"

"That is what you have always been."

"Do you think I'm going to be bossed by you?"

"Ben, if you will tell me just what you want, I shall understand you better," said Lawry, rather impatiently.

"You know what I want. There is only one place in the boat I would be willing to take."

"You mean captain."

"Of course I do."

"I intended to be captain myself."

"I thought you were going to be pilot of her."

"So I am; and captain, too."

"Then you mean to leave me out entirely."

"Ben, I don't want to have any row; and I won't quarrel with my brother; but I don't think it is quite fair for you to ask so much of me."

"Don't I know all about a steamboat?"

"Can you pilot one up and down the lake?"

"Well, no; I never did that kind of work."

"Can you run an engine?"

"No; and you can't, either. The captain doesn't have to be a pilot, nor an engineer."

"What must he do, then?"

"He must look out for everything, make the landing, and see that the people on board are comfortable."

"I intend to do all that."

"How can you do it, and stay in the wheel-house?"

"I shall not stay there all the time. The deck-hands know how to steer. I want to do what's fair and right, Ben. The steamer was given to me; and I don't exactly like to have any one to boss me on board."

"The captain don't have much to do with the pilot, and I sha'n't boss you."

"Suppose the question should come up, whether or not the boat should take a certain job; who would decide the question--you or I?"

"I'm the oldest, and I think I ought to have the biggest voice in the matter."

"But the boat is mine," added Lawry, with emphasis.

"As to that, she is just as much mine as she is yours."

"I'm willing to do what's fair and right; but I shall not have any captain over me in this boat," replied Lawry.

"Lawry, you are my brother," said Ben angrily; "but I don't care for that. You set yourself up above me; you make me a nobody. I won't stand it!"

"I don't set myself up above you, Ben."

"Yes, you do. You offered me the place of deck-hand!"

"I didn't ask you to take any place. I'll tell you what I will do, Ben. I'll talk with mother and Mr. Sherwood about the matter, and if they think you ought to be captain of the *Woodville*, you shall be."

"Mr. Sherwood don't know everything."

"I think he would know what is right in a case like this."

"He thinks you are a little god, and I know what he would say."

"I will do as mother says, then."

"What do women know about these things?"

"I don't think Mr. Sherwood or mother would like it if I should give up the command of this boat to any one."

"Let them lump it, then," replied Ben, as he rushed out of the wheel-house, incensed beyond measure at Lawry's opposition to his unreasonable proposal.

Captain Lawry was sorely disturbed by the conduct of his brother. He could not enjoy his pleasant position at the wheel, and he put the steamer about, heading her toward Port Rock.

"Lawry," said Ben, returning to the wheel-house, "I want you to tell me what you are going to do. I'm older than you, and I have seen more steamboating than you have. I think it's my right to be captain of this boat."

"I don't think so."

"I don't want to jaw any more about it."

"I'm sure I don't."

"All I've got to say is, that if I don't run this boat no one will."

"What do you mean by that, Ben?" demanded Lawry.

"No matter what I mean. I'm going to have what belongs to me. Once for all, am I to be captain, or not?"

"No," replied Lawry firmly.

Ben went out of the wheel-house, and the pilot did not see him again till after the *Woodville* reached her wharf. Lawry was sadly grieved at the attitude of his brother; and if Ben had been a reliable person, fit for the position he aspired to obtain, he would have yielded the point. But the would-be captain was an intemperate and dissolute fellow, as unsuitable for the command as he would have been for the presidency of a bank.

Early on the following morning the supplies for the *Woodville* were taken on board, and at eight o'clock everything was in readiness for the reception of Mr. Sherwood's party. The steam was merrily hissing from the escape-pipe; Ethan was busy, as he always was, in rubbing down the polished parts of the engine, and Lawry was walking up and down the forward deck. Quite a collection of people had assembled on the unfinished wharf and the shore to witness the departure of the steamer. As Captain Lawry paced the deck, there was a slight commotion in the crowd, and three persons passed through, making their way to the deck. One of them was the sheriff who had arrested the ferryman a few days before. He was followed by Mr. Taylor, his father's creditor, and Ben Wilford.

"I'm sorry to trouble you, Lawry," said the official; "but I suppose I must do my duty."

"What's the matter, sir?" asked Lawry. "What have I done?"

"Nothing, my boy. I think this is rather mean business; but I can't help it," replied the sheriff, as he produced certain documents. "Your father owes Mr. Taylor a note of nine hundred and fifty dollars, on which the interest has not been paid for two years, making the debt ten hundred and sixty-four dollars."

"But the place is mortgaged for that," replied Lawry.

"I have just foreclosed the mortgage; and now I must attach this steamboat."

"Attach it!" groaned Lawry.

"Such are my orders; your father's place would hardly sell for enough to pay the debt."

"But this boat is mine," pleaded Lawry.

"You are a minor, Lawry; and your father is entitled by law to all your earnings, as you have a claim on him for your support. I can't stop to explain this matter. The steamer is in my possession now, subject to the decree of the court. I shall appoint a person to take charge of her and run her for the benefit of the parties in interest."

"That's too bad!" exclaimed Lawry.

"I know it is; but I can't help it," replied the sheriff. "I shall appoint your brother, and from this time he has full control of her."

It was evident even to Lawry, who had not been informed of his brother's worst intentions, that Ben was at the bottom of this conspiracy. Such was indeed the truth. Mr. Taylor was a young man who had recently inherited a large fortune, which, it was plain, would soon be squandered, for he was both intemperate and reckless. Ben had helped him home one night after a drunken carousal, which had been the beginning of an intimacy between them, for the younger tippler was not one to neglect an opportunity to secure a wealthy friend.

They had talked together about the **Woodville** on several occasions, and Ben had suggested in what manner he might obtain the debt due him. On the night before the visit of the sheriff to the steamer, the malignant and jealous brother had repeated to his dissipated patron the story of his grievances--that he was a "nobody" at home, and that Lawry wanted to make a deck-hand of him. Though not a badly disposed man in the main, Taylor listened with interest and sympathy to the exaggerated and distorted narrative, and the plan by which Ben was to be put in possession of the steamer was matured.

The creditor went to a lawyer, one of his boon companions, who was quite willing to make business for himself; and he had looked up the law and arranged the facts, by which he expected to hold the steamer. Doubtless it was a very ingenious scheme, and perhaps it is unfortunate that the case never came to trial, for it involved some interesting legal points. Thus far the design had been carried out, and Ben was in command of the steamer, as an employee of the sheriff.

"I won't be as hard with you, Lawry, as you were with me," said Ben, as he walked up to Lawry in the wheel-house, to which he had retreated to hide his confusion.

"This is your work, Ben," replied the youth bitterly.

"I was bound to have the command of this steamer, and I have got it," added Ben, with malignant triumph.

"I know you have; you put Mr. Taylor up to this, or he never would have done it."

"Don't snarl about it, Lawry; the thing is done, and you can't help yourself. The sheriff has given me the command of the boat."

"And he has attached the place. Mother will be turned out of house and home!" cried Lawry, unable to repress his tears.

"No, she won't; that will be all right."

"Oh, Ben! How could you do it?"

"You drove me to it. It is all your fault, Lawry; so you needn't whine about it. Don't make a fuss; here comes Taylor."

"I don't want to see him," said Lawry, moving toward the door.

"Don't go off; I'm going to take Taylor and his friends up the lake, to give them a sail."

"The boat is engaged to Mr. Sherwood, to-day."

"I can't help it; he will not have her to-day. Come, Lawry, be a man. I won't be as hard with you, I say, as you were with me. I don't ask you to be a deck-hand. You shall be the pilot still."

"No, I won't."

"Won't you?"

"I will not," said Lawry firmly, as he dried his tears. "The boat is engaged to Mr. Sherwood, and he has invited a party to go with him. They were to start at nine o'clock, and they will be down here soon."

"Can't help it. I promised to take Taylor and his friends out, and they are all here now. There are the stores for his party," replied Ben, as a couple of men brought a large basket on board, from the top of which protruded the necks of a demijohn and several bottles.

"I shall not go with that party," added Lawry.

"But I want a pilot," said Ben.

"What's the trouble, Wilford?" demanded Taylor.

"Let me tell him you will go, Lawry?" whispered Ben. "He may be hard on you if you don't."

"I will not. I must see Mr. Sherwood at once."

"What's the matter?" asked Ethan.

Lawry was explaining what had happened, when Ben came down with Taylor.

"I shall not go in her till I have seen Mr. Sherwood," added Lawry, as he finished his brief statement.

"Then I shall not," said Ethan.

"I can steer her myself," said Ben to Taylor.

"Certainly you can."

"Mr. Sherwood will be down soon, and we must be off before he gets here."

"Go up, and start her then," added Taylor.

Without noticing Lawry and Ethan, Ben rushed up to the wheel-house, and ordered the deck-hands to cast off the fasts, which was done. He knew how to steer a boat, and understood the bells, having had considerable experience on board the large steamers. He rang to back her, supposing Ethan was at his post in the engine-room.

She did not back, and he rang again, but with no better success than before.

"Back her!" shouted he, through the speaking-tube.

There was no answer; and, filled with anger, the new captain rushed down to the engine-room to "blow up" the engineer. He found Ethan on the main-deck.

"What are you doing there?" demanded Ben. "Don't you hear the bells?"

"I heard them," replied Ethan quietly.

"Why don't you start her, then?"

"I've nothing to do with her."

"Don't you run that engine?"

"I don't."

"What do you mean?"

"I mean that I will have nothing to do with the engine as things are now."

Ben raved and stormed at Ethan; then he tried to coax him to take his place; but the engineer was as firm as the pilot had been. Taylor offered him ten dollars if he would run the engine that day; but he positively refused. The new captain then went down to the fire-room, where the man in charge of the furnaces was promoted to the position of engineer.

"Now we can go it," said Ben.

"No; don't start her," said the sheriff.

"Why not?"

"I am responsible for the safety of this boat, and she shall not go with neither pilot nor engineer."

Taylor and the new captain swore terribly; but the sheriff was immovable.

CHAPTER XVI
THE EXCURSION TO WHITEHALL

Lawry was no lawyer, and was therefore unable to form an opinion in regard to the legality of the steps by which the *Woodville* had been taken from him. It was an accomplished fact, and he was as disconsolate as though he had lost his best friend. He went on shore, and until the peremptory order of the sheriff was given, he expected to see the steamer shoot out from the wharf and disappear beyond the point, in charge of another person than himself.

He had refused to pilot the steamer under the new order of things, not because he wished to be spiteful to his brother, but because he was smarting under a sense of injustice, which unfitted him for the duty. Though he did not comprehend the legal measures which had been taken, he felt that there was something wrong. The *Woodville* belonged to him, not to his father; and though he was willing to give all his earnings for the support of the family, and even to pay off the mortgage on the place, he felt that it was not right to take the steamer from him.

He stood on the wharf, paralyzed by the calamity which had overtaken him. He wanted to do something, but he did not know what to do. The sheriff, by his caution, had defeated the plans of the new captain, and Lawry was waiting to see what would happen next. He wished to see Mr. Sherwood, and he would have hastened up to his house if he could have endured the thought of losing sight of the steamer even for a moment. Ethan was still on deck, for though he refused to run the engine, he felt it to be his duty to stand by and see that no accident happened, for the steam was up, and the fireman was an unskillful person.

Ben Wilford and Taylor were disappointed and chagrined at their failure to get off. They stormed and swore, till it was apparent that storming and swearing would not start the steamer. The sheriff positively refused to let the boat depart without a competent pilot and engineer.

"What shall we do, Wilford?" said Taylor. "Can't you persuade your brother to take hold again?"

"He's as obstinate as a mule; but I'll try," replied Ben.

"Offer him twenty dollars for his day's work," added Taylor.

"I may be able to compromise with him, if you're willing."

"Anything you please, if you can make him and the other fellow go with us."

"Lawry, Mr. Taylor will give you twenty dollars if you will pilot the steamer to-day," said Ben.

"I wouldn't go for a hundred," replied the young pilot. "I won't go with you at any rate."

"Don't be so obstinate, Lawry."

"I engaged the boat to Mr. Sherwood, and I will not go with anybody else."

"Mr. Sherwood won't care when he finds out that you are not to blame. You can't resist the law, and it isn't your fault."

"Ben, I wouldn't do what you have done for all the steamers on the lake. You have got this man to attach the property, and take the house away from mother, just because you wanted to be captain of this steamer."

"What's the use of talking about that, Lawry?" replied Ben impatiently. "I'm going to be captain of this steamer, anyhow; and the sooner you make up your mind to it, the better it will be for you."

"I can't help myself."

"I know you can't, and for that reason you had better submit with a good grace. If you will take your place in the wheel-house, Mr. Taylor will remove the attachment."

"Will he?"

"I will," replied Taylor.

"And put everything where it was before?" asked Lawry.

"Of course I am to be captain, and Mr. Taylor is to have the boat to- day," added Ben.

"Mr. Taylor can't have her to-day," said Lawry firmly. "I engaged her to Mr. Sherwood, and if anybody has her to-day, he must. That's all I want to say about it now."

The young pilot turned on his heel and walked away. His brother and the creditor were conspirators, and he wanted nothing to do with them. He might have been less resolute, if he had not seen Mr. Sherwood's carriage stop at the head of the wharf.

"Are you all ready, Lawry?" asked Mr. Sherwood.

The poor boy could make no reply; he burst into tears, and turned away from his kind friend.

"What's the matter, Lawry?" demanded Mr. Sherwood.

"I suppose he feels bad, sir," interposed the sheriff. "The boat has been attached for his father's debts."

"For his father's debts!" exclaimed the rich gentleman.

The officer gave him a full explanation of the case.

"This will never do," added Mr. Sherwood indignantly. "This boat is Lawry's property in his own right."

"I think not," added Taylor. "Here's my lawyer; he can explain the matter to you."

"No explanation is needed," replied Mr. Sherwood.

"The boy is a minor," said the legal gentleman.

"He may need a guardian, nothing more, to enable him to hold the property."

"Perhaps you are more familiar with the law than I am, Mr. Sherwood," said the legal gentleman pompously. "You gave this boat to the boy."

"I did."

"While she lay at the bottom of the lake she was worth nothing. She was an abandoned wreck. If you had any property at all in her, it was subject to the salvage. Lawry Wilford raised her. I suppose you are willing to believe that the boy's father is entitled to his earnings?"

"I grant that."

"Well, sir, whatever the boy earned in the way of salvage belongs to his father; and we sue to recover that."

"This is a ridiculous suit!" exclaimed Mr. Sherwood.

"Perhaps it is, sir, but we shall hold the boat, subject to the decision of the court."

Mr. Sherwood was vexed and perplexed; for, whether the claim could be substantiated or not, the *Woodville* could be held until a decision was reached. Lawry then took him aside, and told him what his brother had done, in order to make himself captain of the steamer.

"Is that it, Lawry? I'm more sorry for your brother's sake than I am for yours. I pity him, because he has been capable of doing so mean a thing. Don't distress yourself, my boy. We will make this all right in the course of ten minutes."

"But they have taken the steamer away from me, and given her up to Ben, who is to take charge of her."

"Never mind, Lawry. They shall give her back to you," replied the rich man, as he walked up to the lawyer. "How much is your claim against Mr. Wilford?"

"One thousand and sixty-four dollars," answered the legal gentleman.

"Will you take my draft or check for the amount?"

"No, sir."

"I see you are not disposed to be accommodating."

"We intend to have the first sail in this steamer," sneered Taylor.

"I intend you shall not," said Mr. Sherwood.

Unfortunately he had not money enough with him to discharge the claim against the ferryman, which, as it was a just debt, whatever might be said of the means taken to recover it, he had decided to pay, rather than give bonds for the steamer, and contest the attachment. He had invited several gentlemen to accompany him up the lake in the *Woodville*, who were now on the wharf, and from them he borrowed enough to make up the sum required. The money was given to Mrs. Wilford, with instructions to go to a certain lawyer and employ him to see that the mortgage on the house and land was properly canceled.

"When we get our money, the attachment on the boat can be dissolved, not before," said the lawyer. "Mr. Sheriff, the debt is not paid yet."

"I will put the money in your hands, if you desire," added Mr. Sherwood to the sheriff.

"I am satisfied. You may go where you please with the boat, and as soon as you please," replied the official.

"She will not go till this claim is settled, Mr. Sheriff," remonstrated the legal gentleman.

"She may go now," responded the officer. "Ben Wilford, your services will not be needed. Now, gentlemen, we will go up to the village and settle the bills."

The lawyer protested that the attachment could not be removed till the debt had been paid, but the sheriff was willing to take the responsibility of releasing the boat.

"All aboard, Lawry!" shouted Mr. Sherwood.

"I didn't expect you to do this, sir," said the young pilot; "but I will pay you every dollar, if the steamer ever earns so much."

"We will talk about that some other time, my boy. We are all ready to be off now."

Lawry, with a light heart, sprang to his place in the wheel-house; Ethan was already at his post in the engine-room, and the ladies and gentlemen of the party hastened on board.

"Put that basket ashore," said Lawry to the deckhands, as he pointed to the "stores" of the party.

The basket was tumbled on the wharf, to the imminent peril of the glassware it contained. Ben Wilford stood on the pier, leaning against one of the posts to which the steamer was fastened. He looked sour and disappointed.

"Cast off the bow-line," said Lawry, when all was ready.

At this moment Ben jumped on board.

"Stop her!" said Mr. Sherwood sharply, as Lawry rang the bell to back her.

"What's the matter, sir?" asked the pilot.

"Young man," said Mr. Sherwood, stepping up to Ben Wilford, "you will oblige me by going on shore."

"What for?" demanded Ben crustily.

"We do not need your company."

"But I want to go."

"I do not wish you to go."

"I think it is rather steep for you to tell me I can't go in my brother's boat."

"Steep as it may seem, you can't go," added Mr. Sherwood firmly.

"Can't I go, Lawry?" continued Ben.

"It is not for him to say. I have engaged this boat for my party to-day, and, beyond his crew, it is not for him to say who shall go."

"I'm going, anyhow," replied Ben stubbornly.

"No, you are not."

"Yes, I am! if you want to fight, I'm all ready."

"Young man, you wanted to be captain of this boat; you have made a mistake."

"No, I haven't. You and Lawry can't make a nobody out of me."

"You will do it yourself."

"You see."

"Will you go on shore?"

"No, I won't."

The sheriff stood on the wharf with Mrs. Wilford, waiting to see the departure of the *Woodville*. Ben's mother begged him to come on shore; but he was in that frame of mind which seemed to make opposition a necessity to him. "Do you want any assistance, Mr. Sherwood?" asked the sheriff, as he stepped on deck.

The reckless young man would have been very glad to have Mr. Sherwood put his hand upon him, for it would have afforded him an opportunity to revenge himself for his disappointment. It was another thing to raise his hand against an officer of the law, and he sullenly walked up the gangplank when that formidable individual intimated his readiness to relieve the boat of her unwelcome passenger.

"Haul in the plank, and cast off the bow-line," said Lawry.

He rang the bell to back her, and when her bow pointed out from the shore, the stern-line was cast off, and she moved slowly away from the wharf.

"I'm sorry your brother behaves so badly, Lawry," said Mr. Sherwood, after the steamer started.

"It makes me sick to think of it, sir," replied the pilot. "I'm really afraid of him, for I don't know what he will do next."

"Do your duty, faithfully; that is all you need do."

"I feel almost sorry I didn't let him be captain, when I think the matter over."

"He is not fit to be captain; and you did quite right in not consenting to it. I'm sorry for you, Lawry, and sorry for your mother, for he must be a sore trial to both of you."

"If he wasn't my brother I wouldn't care," added Lawry, restraining the tears.

"Never mind it, my boy; we won't say anything more about it. Let us hope your brother will grow better."

"I hope he will, sir."

The *Woodville* was now going at full speed up the lake. The party on board consisted of twenty-four ladies and gentlemen, most of whom were summer visitors at Port Rock. They were delighted with the beautiful little craft, and glad to know that she could be obtained for pleasure-parties during the summer. They wandered about the deck, saloon, and cabin till they had examined every part of her, and then they gave themselves up to the enjoyment of the sail, and of the magnificent scenery on the borders of the lake. They seated themselves on the forward deck, and Lawry pointed out the objects of interest as the steamer proceeded; and in this occupation he forgot the conduct of Ben, and was as happy as the happiest of the party before him. The ladies and gentlemen sang songs and psalm tunes, in which the sweet voice of Fanny Jane Grant was so prominent that Ethan was once enticed from the fascinating engine which occupied all his thoughts.

In the meantime, Mrs. Light was busy with the dinner. Captain Lawry was a little uneasy on this subject, for it was out of his line of business. In the middle of the forenoon he gave the wheel to one of the deck-hands, and went down into the kitchen to satisfy himself that this important matter was receiving due attention. The cook was so confident and enthusiastic that he was quite sure she would realize the expectations of the passengers. In the cabin he found the girls busy at the tables. Both of them had seen service in hotels, and there was no danger of a failure in their department. At one o'clock dinner was on the table, and the young captain went down again to assure himself that it was all right.

"Come, Lawry, can't you dine with us?" said Mr. Sherwood, when the bell had been rung.

"I can't leave the wheel, sir."

"But don't you want some dinner?"

"I'll have my dinner when we get to Whitehall. Haste makes waste, you know; and if I should be in a hurry to eat my dinner we might get aground, or be smashed up on the rocks."

"I suppose you are right, Lawry, and I will do the honors of the table for you," laughed Mr. Sherwood.

The dinner was not only satisfactory, but it was warmly praised; and Mrs. Light was made as happy as the captain by the enthusiastic encomiums bestowed upon her taste and skill in the culinary art.

The *Woodville* reached Whitehall at two o'clock, where the party went on shore to spend an hour. While they were absent Lawry and all hands had their dinner, the cabins and the deck were swept, and everything put in order. Quite a number of people visited the little steamer while she lay at the pier; and a gentleman engaged her to take out a party the next Saturday, with dinner for twenty-four persons. When Mr. Sherwood returned, he had let her for another day.

At three o'clock the *Woodville* started for Port Rock. The party were still in high spirits, and the singing was resumed when the wheels began to turn. On the way down, she stopped at Ticonderoga, while her appearance so delighted a party of pleasure- seekers that she was engaged for another day, and a dinner for twenty spoken for.

"Lawry, you must have an engagement-book, or you will forget some of your parties," said Mr. Sherwood, who stood by the pilot, in the wheel-house, when the steamer started.

"I have put them all down on a piece of paper, sir. I will get a book when I go to Burlington."

"Which will be to-morrow. I had engaged her for four days when you came up with her from Port Henry; but I'm afraid we shall work you too hard."

"No fear of that, sir. I only hope I shall be able to pay you that money you advanced this morning."

"Don't say a word about that. Let me see: you are engaged in Burlington to-morrow, to me the next day, and in Whitehall on the following day."

"I will get a book and put them down, sir."

"But you must be in Burlington by eight o'clock tomorrow morning."

"We can run up to-night."

"You will get no sleep if you run all night."

"I think we shall want another fireman."

"You will: for in order to keep your engagements you will occasionally have to run nights."

At eight o'clock the *Woodville* landed her passengers at Port Rock, and as the gentlemen went ashore, they gave three cheers for the little steamer and her little captain.

CHAPTER XVII
BURLINGTON TO ISLE LA MOTTE

On his way home, Mr. Sherwood went to the ferry-house and satisfied himself that the mortgage on the place had been canceled. Mrs. Wilford was profuse in the expression of her gratitude to him for his kindness to the family, and hoped that Lawry and his father would be able to pay him back the whole sum.

"Mrs. Wilford, so far as gratitude and obligation are concerned, the balance is still largely against me. Millions of dollars would not pay the debt I owe to your son."

"Oh, Lawry don't think anything of that, sir!"

"But I do. Madam, if your son had been five minutes later than he was when the little steamer went down, Miss Fanny Grant would certainly have been drowned, and my wife would doubtless have shared her fate. And when I think that this exposure of their precious lives was my own fault; that my wife and her sister had nearly perished by my foolish haste and recklessness, I feel like giving every dollar I have in the world to Lawry. You don't understand this matter as I do, Mrs. Wilford."

"I didn't think you were in any great danger."

"Miss Fanny would certainly have been drowned; and I don't think it would have been possible for me to save my wife, for I was nearly exhausted when Lawry came. Now, Mrs. Wilford, do you suppose I shall mind one, two, or ten thousand dollars, where my brave deliverer is concerned? In one word, I will never take a dollar which I have expended for Lawry or the family. Your son is a manly and independent boy, and I don't like to hurt his feelings; so I shall not say anything about this money at present."

"Lawry is a good boy," said Mrs. Wilford proudly.

"He is worth his weight in gold. I am sorry your oldest son is not more like him."

"I don't know what to think of Benjamin."

"Where is he now?"

"I don't know; I haven't seen him since the steamer left, this morning."

"Lawry is a good deal troubled about the ferry-boat."

"He needn't be."

"Can you hire a man to run the boat?"

"Yes; I can get a boy who will do it for half a dollar a day, and be glad of the chance. I will engage one."

"Lawry goes to Burlington to-night to take out a party to-morrow."

"To-night?"

"Yes; he must be there by eight in the morning."

Mrs. Wilford thought her son was having a hard time with the steamer; but she knew he would be satisfied as long as he was doing well. Mr. Sherwood, assured that there was nothing at home to detain the young pilot, left the house. Lawry soon after entered; but he had not time to tell his mother the particulars of his first trip on the *Woodville*. He could remain but a few moments, while the hands were "coaling up," from a cargo of coal deposited on the wharf that day, by the order of Mr. Sherwood.

At nine o'clock everything was ready for the departure. The fireman grumbled at being called upon to work at night; but Lawry promised to get another man to keep watch as soon as he could. It was a long day's work for all hands. When the young captain had gone to the wheel-house to start the boat, Mr. Sherwood rushed down the wharf, and jumped aboard.

"I was afraid I should be too late," said he, as Lawry met him on the main-deck. "I have been all over the village to find you another fireman, and I have succeeded in getting you a first-rate one--an old hand at the business."

"Thank you, sir; you are taking a great deal of trouble for me."

"There's another thing I quite forgot; I didn't pay you for the trip nor the dinners. Here is the money."

"I can't take it, Mr. Sherwood," protested Captain Lawry.

"But you must take it; if you don't I can't engage the boat again."

"Not from you, sir."

"I am more interested than any other person in your success with the steamer, and I insist that you take the money."

"I owe you for this cargo of coal, now."

"That was a present from Miss Fanny Grant."

"She is very generous."

"Generous! If she doesn't do more than that for you, I shall be ashamed of her. By the way, captain, she paid the bill for repairing the steamer at Port Henry."

"Indeed!" exclaimed Lawry, who had intended to discharge this debt with the first money he earned. "She is very kind. I don't deserve so much from her and you."

"More, my boy. We haven't done anything at my house but talk about you for a week. Now, you must be reasonable. We intended to give you a good start. Miss Grant wishes to put an upright pianoforte in the saloon. There is just room for it at the end of the stateroom on the starboard side. When that is put in, we shall let you alone. Now, Lawry, take this money; if you don't, I shall be offended."

"I don't like to do so," pleaded Lawry. "It makes me feel mean."

"It need not; take it, Lawry, for you will want money to provision your boat in the morning."

Captain Lawry took it, though it seemed to burn his fingers.

"Now, my boy, you shall have your own way. I will force nothing more on you, except what I fairly owe you, and you shall make your fortune without any help or hindrance from anybody."

"I owe you now---"

"Silence, Lawry!" laughed Mr. Sherwood. "There comes your second fireman."

As the man came down the gangplank, he handed Mr. Sherwood a long package, done up in brown paper.

"One thing more, Lawry," said his munificent friend, as he led the way to the engine-room, which was lighted by a lantern. "Will you let me put this sign up over the front windows in the wheel-house?"

"Certainly, sir. What is it?"

"It is the motto of the steamer, and fully explains how I lost the boat," replied

Mr. Sherwood, as he unrolled the package.

It was a small sign, about three feet in length, elegantly painted and gilded, on which was the motto:

HASTE AND WASTE.

"While you were at Port Henry, repairing the boat, I went up to Burlington, where I ordered this to be done. It came down to-day, and I want it put up in the wheel-house, where it will be constantly before your eyes, as the best axiom in the world for a steamboat man. It will be the history of the **Woodville** to you, and I hope you will always act upon it, never running your boat above a safe speed, nor leave your wharf when it is imprudent to do so."

"I shall be very glad to have those words always before me," replied Lawry.

"When you are ready to go, captain, we are," said Mr. Sherwood.

"I'm all ready, sir."

Lawry turned, and to his astonishment saw Mrs. Sherwood and Miss Fanny, who had been looking over his shoulder at the pretty sign.

"We are going with you, Captain Lawry," added Mr. Sherwood; "that is, if you won't charge us anything for our passage."

"I am very happy to have you as passengers," stammered Lawry.

"We are so much in love with your boat, Lawry, that we could not stay away from her," added Mrs. Sherwood.

"And her captain," said Miss Fanny.

Lawry was good for nothing at complimentary speeches, and he went aft to give the girls directions to light up the cabin and the two staterooms for the accommodation of his unexpected passengers.

"Where's Fanny Jane?" asked Ethan, when Mr. Sherwood had gone to the wheel-house to put up the motto.

"She is going to keep house for us while we are gone," replied Miss Fanny mischievously. "You were so unsocial to-day she would not come with us."

"I had to look out for the engine," pleaded Ethan.

"That was not the reason, Ethan," interposed Mrs. Sherwood. "You behaved splendidly."

"If you were twenty, instead of sixteen, Ethan, I should say you were in love with Fanny Jane," laughed Miss Fanny.

"Oh, nonsense!" exclaimed Ethan, blushing beneath his smutty face. "I like her, and after what we went through out West, I don't think it is very strange I should."

"You are right, Ethan. She is a good girl, and I hope you will like her more, rather than less."

"The saloon is ready for you, ladies," said Lawry, interrupting this pleasant conversation--very pleasant to Ethan, for without entering into an analysis of the young engineer's feelings, it is quite certain he thought a great deal of the companion of his wanderings in Minnesota; but fortunately he is not the hero of this book, and this interesting suggestion need not be followed out any further.

The little captain conducted the ladies to the saloon, and then hastened to the wheel-house, where Mr. Sherwood, by the light of a lantern in the hands of one of the boys, had screwed up the sign.

"Haul in the plank!" shouted Lawry, "Cast off the bow-line."

The *Woodville* backed till she was dear of the wharf, and then went ahead. Lawry knew the lake by night as well as by day, and he was perfectly at home at the wheel, not withstanding the darkness that lay in the steamer's path. One of the deck-hands was a boy of sixteen, who had served in a similar capacity on board the lake steamers, and was a good wheelman, though he knew nothing of the navigation of the lake, and steered only by the directions given him from time to time. Captain Lawry called this hand, and gave him the wheel, with orders to run for a certain headland several miles distant.

The young captain went below with Mr. Sherwood, to make his arrangements for the night. The second fireman had already been installed in the fire-room by Ethan, and the first had gone forward. A portion of the forehold of the steamer had been fitted up for the accommodation of the crew. It contained four berths, and was well ventilated by a skylight in the forecastle. In building the boat, Mr. Sherwood had insisted upon having everything put into her that was to be found in larger craft; and these quarters for the hands were now very convenient, if not indispensable.

Lawry gave one of these berths to the first fireman, and appropriated the other to the use of the second and the two deck- hands. The second boy was gaping fearfully on the forward deck, and was quite delighted when the captain told him he might turn in. On the starboard side of the steamer, forward of the wheels, were two very cunning little staterooms, the corresponding space on the port side being occupied by the kitchen and storerooms. One of these was for the engineer, and the other for the captain. Abaft the wheels, on each side, was a small stateroom, one of which had been designed for the captain. Both of these rooms had been appropriated to the cook and the two waiter girls. Mrs. Light, in the apartment of the commander, was quite delighted with her accommodations; but Mr. Sherwood declared that she deserved a princely couch for the good dinner she had served that day.

The two staterooms to be occupied by the passengers were taken out of the space that would otherwise have been park of the saloon, and were entered by doors on each side of the passageway leading to it. They were beautiful little rooms, though ladies in full crinoline might have been somewhat perplexed at their contracted dimensions. They were elegantly furnished, and Miss Fanny declared that her room made her think of the fairy palaces for little people, of which she had read in her childhood. There were twelve berths in the lower cabin, but these were not needed.

Having disposed of his crew for the night, Lawry returned to the wheel-house, where he was soon joined by his passengers, who spent an hour with him before they retired. At half-past ten they went to their rooms, and Lawry was alone. Not a sound was to be heard except the monotonous clang of the engine, and the lake was as silent in the gloom as though the shadow of death was upon it. There was a solemnity in the scene which impressed the young pilot, even accustomed as he was to the night and the silence. He was worn out by the labors and the excitement of the day, but he could not resist the inspiration which came from the quiet waters and the gloomy shores.

The **Woodville** sped on her way, and at midnight she was approaching the steamboat wharf at Burlington. Lawry rang to "slow down," and informed Ethan that the boat was close to the wharf. The "fires were drawn," and in a few moments more the steamer was made fast to the wharf. After satisfying himself that everything was secure on board, the exhausted pilot went to his stateroom, and was soon fast asleep. Ethan followed him, after instructing the first fireman to get up steam early in the morning.

Both the pilot and the engineer slept till seven o'clock; but when they came out of their rooms, blaming themselves for sleeping so late, they found the decks washed down, the cabins in order, steam up, and breakfast ready. Those who had "turned in" early had faithfully performed the duties belonging to them, as they had been instructed the evening before. Mrs. Light, who was steward as well as cook, had been to the market, and purchased the supplies for breakfast and dinner. Mr. Sherwood and the ladies had risen early, and taken a walk, which gave them a keen appetite for the excellent breakfast prepared for them. The passengers insisted that Captain Lawry should sit at the head of the table with them, as this was the proper place for the commander of the steamer.

During his walk Mr. Sherwood had purchased three blank books, and a double slate, for which Lawry, agreeably to the arrangement that nothing more should be forced upon him, paid the cash on the spot, to the great amusement of the ladies. The memoranda of each trip, including the time of arrival and departure, and of reaching or passing the principal points on the lake, were to be entered on the slate in the wheel-house, and afterward copied into the largest of the blank books. These were called the log-slate and the log-book. The second was the engagement-book, and the third an account-book, in which the receipts and expenses of the steamer were to be kept.

After breakfast Mr. Sherwood assisted his young friend in opening these books, and explained to him the best method of keeping his accounts. By this time the party for the day's excursion had begun to arrive. The ladies and gentlemen were friends of Mr. Sherwood, and he and his wife and Miss Fanny were to join them. A small band had been provided for the occasion, consisting of six pieces.

Precisely at eight o'clock the **Woodville** left the wharf, amid the inspiring strains of the "Star-spangled Banner," performed by the band. The scene was in the highest degree exhilarating; and the little captain was the happiest person on board, where all was merriment and rejoicing. The boat was to go down the lake as far as Isle La Motte, where the party would spend a couple of hours on shore, and return by six o'clock in the afternoon. This program was carried out to the letter, without any accident, or any nearer approach to one than a thunder-shower and squall. When the little captain saw the tempest coming down upon him, he put the boat about and run her up into the teeth of the squall. The ladies and gentlemen saw the commotion on the water, and some of them were very much alarmed; but the *Woodville*, under the good management of Lawry, did not careen a particle, being headed into the wind.

In three minutes it was over, the steamer returned to her former course, and the party wondered that she made no more fuss about it. While the rain continued, the excursionists were compelled to remain in the saloon; but they were full of glee, after their terror had subsided, and the shower was hardly regarded as a detriment to the pleasure of the trip.

At the appointed hour the *Woodville* was at the wharf in Burlington. Before the party left the boat, they met in the saloon, and passed a vote of thanks to the little captain, in which the dinner, the steamer, and her commander were warmly praised. It was written out, a copy was given to Lawry, and it was to be published in the Burlington papers. While the boat was stopping at the wharf, Mr. Sherwood went up to a printing office, where he had left an order for a job in the morning, and returned bringing with him a few copies of the handbill, which was to announce the *Woodville* more generally to the public. It was posted in various parts of the steamer, and read aloud with mischievous delight by Miss Fanny. It was printed in colors, ornamented with a cut of a steamer, and read as follows:

MOST DELIGHTFUL EXCURSIONS ON THE LAKE!
THE NEW AND SPLENDID MINIATURE STEAMER
WOODVILLE,
Captain Lawrence Wilford,
With elegant and luxurious accommodations for thirty passengers, is now ready to convey pleasure-parties to any part of the lake.

Breakfasts, dinners, and suppers provided on board; and the tables will be supplied with the best the market affords.

Apply by letter, or otherwise, to
CAPTAIN LAWRENCE WILFORD,
Port Rock, N. Y.

By seven o'clock the *Woodville* was under way for Port Rock. Lawry gave the helm to one of the deck-hands, and went below to make some entries in his account-book. He had been paid, that day, fifty dollars for the boat, and thirty dollars for dinners. Mrs. Light had expended twenty-six dollars for provisions and groceries, but he still had one hundred and twenty-eight dollars. It was a large sum of money for a boy of fourteen to have, and he counted it with a pride and pleasure which made him forget the fatigue of his severe labors.

At half-past ten the steamer was moored to her wharf at Port Rock. Mr. Sherwood and the ladies bade the little captain good-night, and went home.

CHAPTER XVIII
TEN THOUSAND IN GOLD

It was fortunate for Lawry that he was able to sleep well in the midst of the excitement in which he lived; otherwise his bodily frame must have yielded to the pressure to which it was subjected. He did not wake till seven the next morning, which invigorated his powers and prepared him for the duties of another day. As soon as he turned out, he went up to see his mother, and gave her a hundred dollars of the money he had earned, reserving the balance for the expenses of the boat.

At nine Mr. Sherwood and his party came on board. It had been his intention to visit Ticonderoga; but business letters which he found waiting his arrival the evening before compelled him to change his destination to Burlington.

Just before the party appeared, Ben Wilford had been seen lounging about the wharf. He had complained bitterly to his mother of the treatment he had received from Lawry, and did not seem to be conscious that he had ever been engaged in a base and mean conspiracy against the peace and happiness of the whole family. Mrs. Wilford had spoken plainly to him, which had only increased his irritation. The little steamer was a sore trial to him, for she was the indication of Lawry's prosperity.

Ben had fully persuaded himself into the belief that he, and not Lawry, ought to be captain of the *Woodville*. She was a family affair, and he could not regard his brother as the actual owner of her. He had imagination enough to understand and appreciate the pleasure of being in command of such a fine craft. His conspiracy had signally failed; in his own choice phrase, Mr. Sherwood "carried too many guns for him," and it was useless to contend against money.

The envious brother had so far progressed in his views as to believe that a subordinate position in the *Woodville* was better than no position at all. He had heard of the fine times the parties had on board of her, of the splendid dinners, and the inspiring music; and he was very anxious to have a situation in her. He was afraid of Mr. Sherwood, and dared not again take his place boldly on board. At a favorable moment, when Lawry and the deck-hands were employed on the after part of the deck, he slipped down the plank and into the forecastle, concealing himself in the berth of one of the firemen. This trick might insure him a passage with the excursion-party, if nothing more.

When the ladies and gentlemen had all arrived, the boat left the wharf, and commenced her voyage down the lake. After she had gone a couple of miles Ben Wilford came out of his hiding-place, and proceeded directly to the wheel-house, feeling that he had nothing to fear from his kind-hearted brother, and hoping to conciliate him before Mr. Sherwood discovered that he was on board. He entered the open door of the wheel-house as coolly as though he belonged there.

"Ben!" exclaimed the little captain, when he saw him. "I didn't know you were on board."

"I didn't mean you should till I got ready," replied Ben.

"I don't know as Mr. Sherwood will like it when he sees you," added Lawry.

"If you like it, he will."

"I'm sure I've no objection to your going with me."

"I knew you hadn't."

"But the steamer belongs to Mr. Sherwood to-day."

"Don't you want some help, Lawry? Mother thinks you are working rather too hard."

"I don't think I shall hurt myself," answered Lawry, laughing; and he was really pleased to find Ben in such good humor. "I don't see that you can help me any."

"I can steer."

"So can Rounds," replied Lawry, referring to the deckhand whom he called to the wheel when he left his post.

"Lawry, you are my brother--ain't you?"

"Of course I am."

"And I am your brother--am I not?"

"Without a doubt you are."

"Then there are two good reasons why we should not quarrel."

"I'm very sure I don't wish to quarrel, Ben," added Lawry earnestly.

"And I'm just as sure I don't," continued Ben. "This is a splendid little boat, and we might make a first-rate thing of it. I still think I ought to be captain of her; but I won't quarrel about that now. I'll take any place you have a mind to give me."

This was certainly very kind and condescending on the part of the elder brother, after what had occurred; and Lawry really felt happy in the excellent spirit which Ben appeared to manifest.

"You might give me a chance as mate, if you like," added Ben, as he perceived the smile on his brother's face.

"I will speak to Mr. Sherwood about it."

"What do you want to speak to him for? Don't you own this boat?"

"I do; but he has been very kind to me, and I want to take his advice when I can. I wish you hadn't got into that scrape the other day."

"What scrape?"

"Why, causing the boat to be attached for father's debts."

"I didn't mean anything by it, Lawry," answered Ben, in apologetic tones. "You must acknowledge that you provoked me to it."

"How, Ben?"

"I can't get it out of my head that I ought to be captain of this boat. I think it would be a good deal better for you, Lawry. Just look at it one minute! You are a pilot, and you have to leave the wheel to see to everything on board. You ought to have nothing to do but to navigate the steamer; while I, as captain, could take the money, see to the dinners, and keep the deck and cabins in good order."

"We get along very well," replied Lawry.

"But it will wear you out in a month. Mother is afraid you will kill yourself, running the boat night and day."

"If you were captain I should have to be in the wheelhouse all the time, just the same."

"Well, I don't insist on it, Lawry," replied Ben, with becoming meekness. "I was only saying what would be best for all concerned."

"I will talk with Mr. Sherwood."

"Whatever you say, he will agree to. Now, give me the wheel, Lawry, and you go and see your passengers."

Ben took hold of the wheel, and the young pilot involuntarily released his grasp on the spokes. The older brother was certainly in a very amiable frame of mind, and it was perfectly proper to encourage him; but there was no more need of a mate than there was of another captain. Rounds, as the older of the two deckhands, now performed the duties of that office. There was no freight to be received and discharged, which the mate superintends; and there was nothing for him to do but attend to the gangplank and the mooring lines, and see that the decks were washed down when required.

Lawry was not quite willing to leave the wheel in charge of his brother, for he was painfully conscious that he could not always be trusted. Ben was not often in so pliable a frame of mind, and the little captain could not help suspecting that he had some object in view which was not apparent, for he had twice declared, that if he was not captain of the *Woodville* no one should be. He was not prepared to believe that Ben would run the boat on the rocks, or set her on fire; but he deemed it prudent to keep his eye on him, and on the course of the steamer.

Ben steered very well, and Lawry left the wheel-house. At the door he met Mr. Sherwood, just as that gentleman had discovered who was at the helm.

"How's this, Lawry? Have you got more help?" asked his friend.

"I didn't know Ben was on board till we were two miles from the wharf. I hope you don't object, sir."

"Certainly not, Lawry. If you are satisfied, I have no reason to be otherwise."

"Ben talks very fair this morning; and I'm sure I don't want to quarrel with him."

"Of course not."

"He still thinks he ought to be captain, and that it would be better for me;" and Lawry stated his brother's argument.

"That's all very pretty," replied Mr. Sherwood. "If you wish to give your brother the command of your steamer, it is not for me to interpose any objection."

"But I want to follow your advice."

"I think you had better let things remain as they are, for the present, at least. Do as you think best, Lawry. I don't want to influence you."

This conversation took place near the door of the wheel-house, and, though the parties had not so intended, Ben heard every word of it.

"Do as you think best, Lawry," continued Mr. Sherwood.

"I want to do what you think is best, sir."

"You know my opinion. Your brother's habits--I am sorry to say it-- are not good. I should not be willing to trust him. You cannot place much confidence in a young man who is in the habit of getting drunk. I don't want to hurt your feelings, Lawry, but I must be frank with you."

Ben ground his teeth with rage, as he listened to this plain description of himself, and, in accordance with his usual practice in such cases, vowed to be revenged upon the man who had traduced him, which was his interpretation of Mr. Sherwood's candid statement of the truth.

"I think you are right, sir," replied Lawry, realizing that Ben was not fit for the command of the **Woodville**, even if he was disposed to give it to him.

"Lawry, I have been compelled to change this excursion into a partial business trip. I am going to buy the surplus-gold of a bank in Burlington, and you must leave me there and go on to Port Kent. On your return, you can stop for me," continued Mr. Sherwood. "What is your engagement for to-morrow."

"At Whitehall, sir."

"Capital! You can convey my gold through, so that I can take the morning train at Whitehall for New York."

"If we get back to Port Rock by six, we can reach Whitehall by twelve."

"Well, that is sooner than I wish to arrive," added Mr. Sherwood thoughtfully. "I shall have ten thousand dollars in gold with me, which, at the present rate, is worth about twenty-five thousand dollars in currency. It would be a great temptation to any rogues, who might find out the specie was on board. How would it do to start from Port Rock at midnight?"

"It will do just as well, sir."

"Then I shall reach Whitehall just in time for the train. But, Lawry, I see that you must have another pilot on board."

"I think I can get along, sir."

"You will wear yourself out. You have run a portion of the last two nights, and this arrangement will make the third."

"I can sleep just as well at Port Rock as at Whitehall. To-morrow will be Saturday, and my engagements for Monday and Tuesday are at the upper end of the lake, so that I shall have no more night work at present. I can stand it well enough."

"I'm afraid it will be too much for you; but if you have to engage an extra pilot, you must raise your price to sixty dollars a day."

"I think we shall need another engineer at the same time. Ethan has just as hard a time of it as I do."

"You had better raise your price; people will not object."

"I was thinking, sir, that Ben would make a good pilot. He is a good wheelman, and it wouldn't take him long to learn the courses on the lake."

Mr. Sherwood shook his head.

"Would you be willing to trust him with the boat?--go to sleep yourself, while he is at the helm?" asked he.

"I think I would, after he had learned the navigation."

"He is your brother, Lawry, and I don't like to say anything to wound you; but I feel that your brother is not a reliable person. You must be very prudent. Even a trifling accident, resulting from mismanagement, might ruin your business; for people will not expose their lives needlessly. If Ben will run the ferry the rest of the year, keep sober, and behave well in every respect, you might make a pilot of him, or even captain, another season."

Doubtless this was good advice, and the little captain had so much confidence in his friend and benefactor that he could not help adopting it. Mr. Sherwood went into the cabin again, without any conversation with the subject of his severe but just comments. Lawry was on the point of leaving the hurricane-deck, where he had talked with his adviser, when he noticed that the boat was headed toward the shore, and in a moment more would be aground in the shoal water off Barber's Point. He rushed into the wheel-house, and found that Ben had abandoned the helm. Grasping the wheel, the pilot brought her up to her course, and then turned to his brother.

"What do you mean, Ben, by leaving the wheel?" demanded Lawry, filled with indignation at his brother's treachery.

"Don't talk to me," growled Ben.

"The boat would have been aground in a minute more."

"I wish she was."

"What's the matter, Ben?"

"I thought you were my brother; but you are not."

"I'm sorry to hear you talk so; and I didn't think you would do so mean a thing as to run the boat ashore."

"I'll do anything now. I heard what Sherwood said to you, and what you said to him. I didn't think you would let any man talk about your brother as he did. Do you suppose I would let any man talk like that about my brother? I'll bet I wouldn't! I'd knock him over before the words were out of his mouth."

"Why, what did he say, Ben?"

"What did he say! Didn't you hear what he said? Didn't he tell you I was a drunken fellow, and couldn't be trusted?"

"Well, he certainly did," replied Lawry moodily.

"And you heard him! And you didn't say a word!" said Ben furiously.

"What could I say when Mr. Sherwood spoke only what I know is true?"

"Then you think I'm a drunken fellow, and can't be trusted?" demanded Ben, with an injured look.

"Don't you drink too much sometimes?"

"No, I don't! I drink what I want; but no one ever saw me the worse for liquor. Who says I can't be trusted?"

"When I gave you the wheel, at your own request, you left it, and the boat would have been ashore in another minute. Does that look as though you could be trusted?" added Lawry.

"That was because you wouldn't trust me. I was mad."

"One who would expose the lives of twenty or thirty persons when he got mad ought not to be trusted."

"Lawry, you are no longer my brother. You and your mother, and Sherwood here, have been trying to put me down, and make a nobody of me. You can't do it. I'm your enemy now. You have made me mad, and you must take the consequences. I'll burn or smash this boat the first chance I get! As for Sherwood, I'll teach him to talk about me!"

The angry young man rushed out of the wheel-house. If Mr. Sherwood had heard his insane threats he would probably have insisted that he should be immediately put on shore; but Lawry did not think his brother capable of the madness of malice his speech indicated; he was in a passion, and when he cooled off he would be reasonable again.

Ben sat down on the forecastle where the pilot could see him, and nursed his wrath till the **Woodville** arrived at Burlington. He was in deep thought all the time, and did not heed the singing or other amusements of the party on board, who were enjoying themselves to the utmost. Apparently with no perception of his own faults and shortcomings, he regarded himself as a deeply injured young man. His mother and his brother had turned against him, and were persecuting him to the best of their ability. He had come on board to gain his purpose by conciliation; he had failed, and, in his own view, there was nothing left for him but revenge.

The boat touched at Burlington, and to the great relief of Lawry, his brother followed Mr. Sherwood on shore. At three o'clock the **Woodville** returned from Port Kent with the happy excursionists. While the steamer lay at the wharf, waiting for Mr. Sherwood, many persons, moved by curiosity to inspect the beautiful craft, came aboard; and whenever she stopped, she had plenty of visitors of this description. Among them Lawry saw his brother, accompanied by two men, who, from the remarks they made, were evidently familiar with the machinery and appointments of steamers.

Mr. Sherwood presently appeared attended by a bank messenger with the precious coin he had purchased at 2.44, the telegraphic quotation from New York for that day.

"Where shall I put this gold. Captain Lawry?" asked Mr. Sherwood.

"I don't know, sir; I'm really afraid of it," replied the captain nervously. "Can't you carry it in your pockets?"

"It weighs about thirty-seven pounds," laughed Mr. Sherwood. "I will lock it up in my stateroom. I shall sleep on board to-night, and it will be safe enough after we leave the wharf, for no one but you and me knows there is any specie on board."

The man of gold went aft with the coin, which was contained in two bags.

"I suppose I can go home with you--can't I, Lawry?" asked Ben, as the little captain started for the wheel-house.

Lawry could not refuse this request, though his brother was evidently a little excited by the liquor he had drank. He hoped Ben had not heard anything about the treasure on board; for he feared that revenge, if not dishonesty, might prompt him to commit a crime.

The visitors were warned ashore, and the *Woodville* departed for Port Rock, where she arrived at about six o'clock. The excursion-party went on shore, after the usual compliments to the steamer and her commander.

"Now, Lawry, I must go up to the house for my valise; but I will return in an hour," said Mr. Sherwood, whose carriage was waiting for him at the head of the wharf.

"But the gold, sir?" whispered Lawry anxiously.

"You or Ethan may watch the stateroom till I return, if you please; but there is no danger here. You must turn in at once, Lawry, so as not to lose your sleep."

"I shall be gone four or five days, this time, and I must go home after some clean clothes."

"Very well; I will get Ethan to keep his eye on the stateroom," replied Mr. Sherwood; and Lawry ran up to the cottage.

Ethan, who had ordered the fires to be banked in furnaces, and was letting off the superfluous steam, consented to watch the room containing the gold. Rounds, the deckhand, and the first fireman turned in, that they might be ready for duty at midnight, when the boat would start for Whitehall.

CHAPTER XIX
CAPTURED AND RECAPTURED

Unfortunately for Ben Wilford, he had heard Mr. Sherwood inform Lawry of his intentions in regard to the purchase and transportation of the gold. Before the *Woodville* reached Burlington, the dissolute young man had resolved to obtain the money if possible, prompted partly by revenge, and partly by the desire to possess so large a sum, with which he could revel in luxury in some distant party of the country. It must be confessed that this resolve to commit a crime was not simply an impulse, for the young man who leads a life of indolence and dissipation is never at any great distance from crime. Ben had been schooling himself for years for the very deed he now determined to do.

With more energy and decision, Ben was, in other respects, the counterpart of his father. His moral perceptions were weak, and the dissolute life he led had not contributed to strengthen them. He was the antipode of Lawry, who had been more willing to listen to the teachings of his mother.

Ben had resolved to commit a crime, but he had not the skill or the courage to do it alone. When he went on shore at Burlington, he met two of his former boon companions, with whom he had often tippled, gambled, and caroused. One of them had been a fireman, and the other a deck-hand, on board a steamer with Ben, and he knew them thoroughly. By gradual approaches he sounded them, to ascertain their willingness to join him in the robbery. The gold converted into currency would give them seven or eight thousand dollars apiece, and the temptation was sufficiently strong to remove all prudential obstacles.

While the *Woodville* was absent on her trip to Port Kent, the details of the robbery had been settled. The confederates sat on the corner of the wharf and arranged their plans, which were mainly suggested by the one who had been a fireman.

The scheme was to be executed while the boat lay at Port Rock, and the two men whom Lawry had seen with his brother were his associates in the intended crime. Ben had concealed them in the forehold of the steamer. While the excursion-party were going on shore at the gangway abaft at the wheels, and all hands had gone aft to witness their departure, Ben had called them from their hiding-place, and sent them on the wharf, where he soon joined them. From a point near the head of the pier, where they were not observed, they waited till Mr. Sherwood and Lawry had gone, and all was quiet on board of the steamer.

"Now is our time," said Ben nervously; for he was not familiar enough with crime to be unmoved by the desperate situation in which he had placed himself.

"Is the coast clear?" asked the fireman.

"Yes," replied Ben, whose teeth actually chattered with apprehension.

"Who is there on board now?"

"No one but the engineer and the fireman, except two boys," answered Ben. "They were all going to turn in as soon as they got to the wharf."

"The firemen are both men, but I reckon they won't fight; all the rest are boys."

"One fireman and two boys have turned in by this time," added Ben.

"Then there is no one up but the engineer and one fireman?"

"No."

"Where is the gold, Ben?"

"In the starboard saloon stateroom."

"All right; have your pistols ready, but don't use them, for it will be bad for us if we have to kill any one."

The party walked down to the *Woodville*. All was still on board of her, except the sound of escaping steam. Ethan stood sentry at the door of the stateroom containing the gold, and the man on watch in the fire-room was busy reading a newspaper. It was not sunset yet, but the crew of the *Woodville* had been worked so hard for three days that those off duty could sleep without an opiate.

"Put on that hatch," said the fireman, who became the leading spirit of the party, as he pointed to the companion-way of the forehold, where the hands slept.

Ben obeyed the order without making any noise, and then the party went aft, where Ethan was keeping guard over the treasure.

"Good evening, Ethan," said Ben, with more suavity than he was in the habit of using.

"Good evening," replied the engineer.

"Haven't turned in yet?" continued Ben.

"No."

"Going to start at midnight, I hear."

"Yes."

"Some friends of mine wanted to look over the boat; I suppose I can show them through."

"I don't know; Captain Lawry can tell you," answered Ethan, who did not like Ben, and was not favorably impressed by the appearance of the other men.

Ben walked aft into the saloon, followed by his companions. Ethan was sitting in a chair by the side of the stateroom door. The fireman passed round behind, and suddenly fell upon him, throwing him on the floor and pinioning his arms to his back.

"What are you about?" cried Ethan, struggling to release himself. "Help! help!"

"Stop his mouth!" said Ben fearfully.

Vainly poor Ethan endeavored to shake off his assailants; his arms were tied together behind him, and a handkerchief stuffed into his mouth. In this condition he was lashed to a stanchion, so that he could move neither hand nor foot.

The commotion of this outrage attracted the attention of Mrs. Light and the two waiter-girls, who were employed in the lower cabin. The fireman exhibited a pistol to them, drove them below again, and threatened to shoot them if they made any noise. A similar demonstration quieted the fireman, and compelled him to return to the fire-room.

"The job is done," said Baker, the leader of the enterprise.

"But we haven't got the money," added Flint, the deckhand.

"We don't want that yet. It is safe where it is. Now both of you to your stations," continued Baker; and he went down into the fire-room.

Ben's station was in the wheel-house, Flint's at the fasts, and Baker's at the engine, as it appeared from their subsequent movements; and it was evident, from the operations in progress, that the villains intended to make their escape in the steamer. Baker stopped the hissing steam which was going to waste, and compelled the fireman to renew the fires.

"Be lively!" shouted Ben, from the wheel-house, as he discovered Lawry on the shore, hastening back to the steamer with his bundle of clothes.

"All ready!" replied Baker, finding there was steam enough to start the boat.

Flint had already cast off the fasts, without waiting for orders, and was standing on the forecastle, as impatient to be off as a man can be who is engaged in the commission of a crime.

Ben rang the bell to back her; the wheels turned, but as the stern-line had been cast off, her bow was not carried out from the wharf. By this time Lawry had discovered that the *Woodville* was in motion. He was astonished and alarmed, though he was far from surmising that his boat had been captured by robbers. Running with all his speed, he reached the head of the wharf just as the boat had backed far enough to permit Ben to see him, and for him to see that Ben was at the wheel. Then he realized that his brother was engaged in another conspiracy.

Notwithstanding his extensive knowledge of "steam-boating" in general, Ben Wilford was a very unskillful pilot. If he had understood the management of a boat half as well as Lawry, the nefarious scheme might have been successful. He saw his brother; he did not wish to have him come on board, for Lawry might be so obstinate as to induce one of his dissolute companions to fire at him. He rang the bell to stop her, and then to go ahead, at the same time putting the helm hard aport.

The *Woodville* went forward, and as she met the helm her bow came round, and she was headed out into the middle of the lake. As she went ahead, her stern swept in a circle within a few feet of the wharf, just as Lawry, breathless with haste and alarm, reached the end of the pier. The little captain knew nothing of the state of things on board, except that his brother Ben was at the wheel, which, however, was a sufficient explanation to him. The *Woodville* was going, and he could not let her depart without him. Dropping his bundle, he leaped to the plankshear, grasping the rail with both hands. Jumping over the bulwark, he stood on the guard from which opened the windows of the saloon.

Neither of the three conspirators were in a situation to see this movement on the part of Lawry. Ben was too much occupied in steering-- for he was not a little fearful of getting aground in some shoal water between the ferry and the wharf-

-to notice anything; but as soon as he had obtained his course, he looked for his brother on the pier. He was not there; but Ben did not suspect that he was on board the *Woodville*. Baker, who knew just enough about an engine to stop and start it, was working the valves with the bar; and he could think of nothing else. Doubtless he was conscious by this time that he had "taken a big job," in assuming the control of the engine.

Lawry was bewildered by the situation. When his feet struck the deck, his first impulse was to rush up to the wheel-house, and confront the difficulty as the case might require. He started to carry out his purpose, when he happened to look through one of the saloon windows, and discovered Ethan, with the handkerchief in his mouth, tied to the stanchion. Deeply as he sympathized with his friend in his unpleasant position, he was still cheered by the sight, for it assured him that the engineer had been faithful to his duties, and was not a party to the conspiracy.

The little captain went round and entered the saloon by the door, without being seen by either of the conspirators. He removed the gag from Ethan's mouth, and proceeded to unfasten the cords with which he was bound.

"What does all this mean, Ethan?" demanded Lawry, in excited tones, and almost crying with vexation.

"Hush! Do they know you are here?" asked the engineer.

"I think not; I don't know."

"Keep still, then. They are after the gold."

"Who are they?"

"Ben and two other fellows. I don't know them."

"We'll stop this thing very quick," said Lawry.

"They are armed with pistols, and threatened to shoot all hands. Be careful, Lawry, or you will get a bullet through your head."

"What shall we do?" demanded the young pilot.

Ethan was an accomplished strategist. He led the way to the lower cabin, where the terrified women had been driven by the ruffians.

"If any of those men ask for me, tell them I got loose, jumped overboard, and swam ashore," said Ethan.

"Law sake!" exclaimed the cook.

"Don't tell them I am here, at any rate."

"I won't. Massy sake! What are we comin' to?"

"Don't be alarmed; we will take care of these villains before we have done with them," added Ethan.

"Hush! There's some one coming," said one of the girls; and the heavy tread of a man was heard on the deck above them.

Ethan and Lawry had only time to crawl into one of the berths, where Mrs. Light covered them with bedclothes, before Flint came down into the cabin.

"See here; we haven't been to supper, and we want some," said the ruffian, as he descended the steps.

"What are you goin' to do with us?" demanded Mrs. Light.

"Don't be scart; we won't hurt you," replied Flint.

"But where you goin'?"

"Up to Whitehall. When we get there, you can go where you please. Now, get us some supper; the best there is on board--beefsteak and coffee."

"Well, I suppose I can get you some supper; but I don't like such carryin's on," replied Mrs. Light.

Flint left the cabin, after he had given his order. On his way forward he looked into the saloon, and discovered that their prisoner was missing. Search was immediately instituted; but Mrs. Light, as instructed by Ethan, declared that he had got loose and swam ashore; she had seen him through the stern-lights. The rascals finally accepted this explanation, after searching on deck for him.

Mrs. Light went to the kitchen to get supper for the rogues, while the girls set the table. The cook presently returned to the cabin, and told Ethan where each of the robbers was stationed; but being unarmed, there seemed to be no way of making an attack upon them where the ruffians could not rally to the support of each other.

"We must settle this business down here, Lawry," said Ethan, when they had come out of their hiding-places.

"They will have to come to supper one at a time," added the little captain.

"Exactly so; and this will be the safest place to do the job. We want a rope," added the engineer, with a businesslike air.

"I'll fetch you a rope," said Mrs. Light.

"Do; bring me the small heave-line, on the guard by the saloon doors."

The cook went on deck, and after a visit to the kitchen, returned to the cabin with the line indicated under her apron. In about half an hour supper was ready for the villains, and one of the girls informed Baker, who was still on duty in the engine-room, that it was waiting for them. The engineer called Flint, and told him, as the boat was out in the middle of the lake, the engine would need nothing done to it, and directed him to stand at the door, so that the fireman below should not attempt to defeat their plans. He then went to the cabin for his supper.

Ethan and Lawry had concealed themselves behind the curtains of a tier of berths, directly in the rear of the chair where Baker was to sit at the table. In his hand Ethan held the heave-line, at one end of which Lawry had made a hangman's noose. Mrs. Light and the girls had been instructed to rattle the chairs, make as much noise as they could, and otherwise engage the attention of the robber, as soon as he sat down to the table.

Baker came down the stairs, and one of the girls began to rattle the chairs, Mrs. Light to move a pile of plates, and the other girl to arrange the dishes on the table. "Will you have some coffee?" demanded Mrs. Light, without giving him time to notice anything in the cabin.

"Of course I will," growled Baker.

"Shall I give you some beefsteak?" asked one of the girls.

"I'll help myself."

"If you want some fried eggs I'll get some for you," added the cook, rattling the dishes again.

Baker was not permitted to say whether he would have any fried eggs or not, for at that moment Ethan crept from his concealment, whatever noise he made being drowned by the clatter of the dishes and the rattling of the chairs. Stealing up behind Baker, who was intent only on beefsteak and coffee, he slipped the hangman's noose over his head, and hauled it tight. The robber attempted to spring to his feet, but Ethan hauled him over backward on the floor. At the same time Lawry threw the end of the line over a deck beam, extended across the skylight, and began to "haul in the slack."

The villain attempted to cry out; but the sound only gurgled in his throat. He grasped the rope with both hands; but the choking already received had taken away his strength, and he was unable to make any successful resistance. While

Lawry kept the rope so taut that Baker could not move, Ethan tied his hands behind him, though the man's struggles were fierce, and the engineer was obliged to use a rolling-pin, supplied by Mrs. Light, before the conquest was complete. The ruffian was securely bound and gagged; but the cook and the girls had nearly fainted while the struggle was going on.

Baker, thus gagged and bound, was rolled into one of the lower berths. He had been nearly choked to death by the rope, and several hard knocks he had received on the head had rendered him partially insensible, so that he was not in condition to make any further resistance. Ethan had taken possession of his pistol, and, as a matter of precaution, threatened to blow out his brains if he made any noise.

"Massy sake!" groaned Mrs. Light. "I never did see! You've taken my breath all away!"

"Don't make a noise," said Ethan.

"I couldn't have struck that man as you did," added Lawry.

"If you had been through what I have, out West, it would come easier to you," replied the engineer. "We must go through the whole of it once more."

One of the girls was then sent to call Flint, and directed to assure him that such was the order of Baker, who had gone to the wheel-house for a moment, and would immediately return to the engine-room. The deck-hand was too much in a hurry for his supper to question the order, and went directly to the cabin. The noise made by Mrs. Light and the girls prevented him from hearing the heavy breathings of Baker, and he was an easier victim than his companion in crime had been. He was choked, gagged, bound, and his pistol taken from him. By this time these two ruffians, if they could think at all, could not help believing that the way of the transgressor is hard.

From regard to the feelings of Lawry, Ethan decided that Ben should not be subjected to this harsh treatment. He was still in the wheel-house, not suspecting that his nefarious scheme had been wholly defeated.

The work was accomplished, and the pilot and engineer went on deck. Ethan repaired to his post and stopped the engine. Ben half a dozen times demanded, through the speaking-tube, what the matter was; but receiving no answer, he came down himself to ascertain the cause of the sudden stoppage of the boat.

CHAPTER XX
THE LITTLE CAPTAIN AND HIS MOTTO

As Ben Wilford, fearful that some accident to the machinery would defeat his criminal enterprise, entered the engine-room on one side, Lawry left it at the other. As the little captain went forward, he heard a noise in the forecastle, and saw that the companionway was closed and fastened. Releasing the firemen and deck-hands confined there, he directed them to follow him to the wheel-house, where he explained to them what had happened.

"What are you stopping for?" demanded Ben Wilford, before he discovered that Baker was not present.

"I think it is about time to go back, now," replied Ethan, holding one of the pistols in his hand.

"How came you here, Ethan?" exclaimed Ben, starting back with astonishment when he saw who was in charge of the engine.

"I run this machine, and this is the right place for me," replied Ethan coolly.

"Where's Baker?"

"He's safe; if you mean the man you left in charge of the engine."

Ben was bewildered by the present aspect of affairs. It was clear that there had been a miscarriage somewhere; but he was unable to tell how or where the scheme had failed. Before he could decide what step to take next, Captain Lawry rang the bell to go ahead.

"Who rang the bell?" asked Ben.

"Captain Lawry."

"Is he on board?"

"He is," replied Ethan, as he started the engine. "Ben Wilford, you have got about to the end of your rope."

"What do you mean?"

"You have done a job which will send you to Sing Sing for the next ten years."

"No, I haven't," said Ben, backing out of the engine-room.

"Stop where you are," interposed Ethan, peremptorily, as he raised his pistol.

"Two can play at that game," added Ben.

"Two can; but two won't. Drop your hands, or I'll fire!"

Ben obeyed; he had felt that the game was up the moment he saw Ethan at his post, and he had not the courage to draw his pistol upon one who had shot two Indians in one day.

"Sit down there," continued Ethan, pointing to the bench in the engine-room, and the culprit took his seat with fear and trembling.

"What shall I do?" groaned the wretched young man, as he thought of the consequence of his crime.

"Jump overboard and drown yourself. That would save your friends a great deal of trouble," replied Ethan. "Give up your pistol!"

Ben gave it up, and began to plead with Ethan to let him escape, declaring that it would kill his mother, and Lawry never would get over it, if he was sent to the penitentiary. Though the engineer dreaded the day when his friend would be compelled to testify in court against his own brother, he would not yield to the culprit's entreaties, and did not intend that he should escape the penalty of his crime.

When the **Woodville** reached her wharf, having been absent but little more than an hour, Mr. Sherwood and the ladies were on the wharf. While Ethan was working the engine with the bar, Ben slipped out of the room. The engineer saw him, and gave the alarm; but he could not leave his post at that moment. As soon as the boat was moored, search was made; but Ben could not be found. He certainly was not on board.

Mr. Sherwood was astonished when he was told what had occurred. He sent his coachman after the sheriff at once, and directed that the search for Ben Wilford should be renewed. The stateroom was found locked, as he had left it, and the gold undisturbed. Mrs. Light and the girls, the firemen and the deck-hands, had their own stories to tell, to all of which Mr. Sherwood listened very patiently.

"You have done well, Lawry," said he. "You have saved my gold."

"It was Ethan, sir, that did the business. I don't believe I could have done anything alone," replied the little captain.

"Lawry did his share," added Ethan, with due modesty.

"I'm sure they both fit like wildcats in the cabin," said Mrs. Light. "I was e'en a'most scart to death."

When the sheriff came, he took Baker and Flint into custody, and sent the constable who had come with him to find Ben Wilford. The two robbers in the cabin were in bad condition. The choking they had received had been a terrible shock to their nerves, which, with the hard knocks given by Ethan with the cook's rolling-pin, had entirely used them up, and there was neither fight nor bravado in them. Flint said they had been induced to engage in the enterprise by Ben Wilford; that they intended to proceed to the vicinity of Whitehall in the *Woodville*, where the instigator of the affair had declared his purpose to burn the boat. From this point they were going to the West, disposing of the gold in small sums as they proceeded.

The two robbers were marched off by the sheriff; but nothing was heard of Ben for two hours, when the boy who ran the ferry-boat, returning from Pointville, informed Mrs. Wilford that he had gone over with him. The constable followed, as soon as he heard in what direction the fugitive had gone. He was not taken that night, and the search was renewed the next day, but with no better result. It was afterward ascertained that he had crossed the country to the railroad, and taken a night train. Having worked his way to New York, he shipped in a vessel bound to the East Indies.

It cannot be denied that Lawry and his mother, and even Mr. Sherwood, were glad of his escape, though he was more guilty than the two men who had been captured and were afterward tried and sent to Sing Sing. The little captain and the engineer of the *Woodville* were warmly congratulated upon the safety of the steamer, when it was known that Ben intended to burn her in revenge for having been made a "nobody"; but Mr. Sherwood declared that, if the boat had been destroyed, he would have built another, and presented her to Lawry and Ethan, for he was too much interested in the steamboat experiment to have it abandoned.

Mrs. Wilford trembled when she learned that the robbers had been armed with pistols. Many laughed as they, listened to the account of the choking operation in the cabin, and everybody was satisfied with the result.

Lawry and Ethan were too much excited to sleep that night, though they turned in at ten o'clock. At midnight the fireman on duty called them, and the steamer soon started for Whitehall with Mr. Sherwood and his gold, where she arrived in season for the morning train. As the party did not start till nine o'clock, the exhausted pilot and engineer obtained a couple of hours' sleep, while the steamer lay at the wharf, which enabled them to get through the day without sinking under its fatigues.

The following day was Sunday; and though Lawry and Ethan went to church in the forenoon, as both of them were in the habit of doing, the day was literally a day of rest to them, and there was a great deal of "tall sleeping" done. On Monday morning, at six o'clock, the boat went to Ticonderoga, arriving in good season to keep her engagement.

Our limits do not permit us to follow Captain Lawry and the beautiful little steamer any farther. The young pilot has redeemed the fairy craft from the bottom of the lake, and overcome all obstacles in his path to prosperity. He was not again disturbed by the envy and jealousy of his brother. He was sad when he thought of his father in prison, and Ben an exile, banished by his misdeeds; but their errors only made him the stronger in the faith he had chosen, that fidelity to principle is the safest and happiest course, under all circumstances.

Lawry had all the business he could do with the *Woodville*. On the following week, another pilot and another engineer were obtained, and the price raised to sixty dollars a day, in conformity with the suggestion of Mr. Sherwood. This was especially necessary, as, during the bright moonlight evenings, in the latter part of the month, the *Woodville* was employed every night in taking out parties. The boat lay hardly an hour at a time at the wharf. The money came in so fast that Mrs. Wilford was bewildered at the riches which were flowing in upon them. By the advice of Mr. Sherwood the money was invested in government stocks; but he resolutely refused to accept payment for what he had advanced on the place or for the boat.

Early one evening, after Lawry had landed Mr. Sherwood's party at Port Rock, he started for Burlington, where he had an engagement on the following day. Half a mile above the wharf, he came up with a schooner, which on examination proved to be the *Missisque*. It was a dead calm, and her new mainsail hung motionless from the gaff. The little captain had not seen her skipper since the day on which the old sail had been blown from the bolt-ropes by the squall; and he ran the Woodville alongside of her, in order "to pass the time of day" with him.

"How are you, Captain John?" shouted the young pilot.

"Why, Lawry! How are you?" replied the skipper of the sloop.

"What are you doing here?" continued Lawry.

"Waitin' for a breeze of wind. I had a good freight promised to me if I got to Burlington by to-morrow morn-in', but I guess I sha'n't quite fetch it."

"Rounds, heave a stern-line to the sloop, and make fast to her," added Lawry to his mate.

"Oh, thank ye, Lawry," replied the grateful skipper.

"You and your wife must take supper with me."

"Well, Lawry, I always knowed you was smart," said Captain John.

"If I didn't get that mainsail down," laughed Lawry.

"Oh, never mind the mainsail, Lawry," added the skipper, blushing. "I was a leetle riled that time, and it wan't your fault."

"I think the green-apple pies made the mischief. Mrs. Light makes very nice ones, and we will have some for supper," continued Lawry, as he conducted his guests to the cabin, where they sat down at the table.

Captain John and his wife were bewildered at the splendors which surrounded them, and at the grandeur of Captain Lawry; but they passed a pleasant evening on board till ten o'clock, when the *Woodville* cast off her "tow" in Burlington Bay.

The upright piano, the gift of Miss Fanny, had been placed in the saloon, and its sweet strains added to the enjoyment of every party that employed the steamer. Ethan French, now relieved of part of his duties by the employment of a second engineer, was never in better humor than when Fanny Jane, seated at this instrument, sang the songs she had sung to Wahena and himself on the lake island in Minnesota.

In September, the business of the *Woodville*, as an excursion boat, began to fall off, and by the middle of the month it was at an end. The season had been very profitable, and Lawry's account-book showed that the boat had been employed forty-one days, besides nine evenings, the net profits of which were nearly fifteen hundred dollars, all of which was in the bank, or invested in government securities.

While Captain Lawry was considering the practicability of running the *Woodville* between certain places on the lake as a passenger-boat, he was startled by receiving a huge government envelope, containing a liberal offer for the use of his steamer as a despatch boat on southern rivers. An army officer, of high rank, who had been a member of one of the excursion parties in August, had been delighted with the performance of the little craft, and had spoken to Captain Lawry on this subject; but the matter had been quite forgotten when the offer came. Mr. Sherwood and Mrs. Wilford were consulted, and an affirmative answer returned. Ethan was delighted at the prospect of going South, for he desired to visit the scene of hostilities, and, if possible, to be employed in active operations.

The *Woodville* went in October, and returned in April, when the war was finished. Of Captain Lawry's voyage out and back, and his adventures far up in the enemy's country, we have no space to speak; but the steamer and her little commander gave perfect satisfaction.

In June, when the *Woodville* had been thoroughly repaired and painted, after her hard service at the South, there was a demand for her as an excursion boat; and it continued through the season. With one of Mr. Sherwood's parties, in July, there was an eminent member of the State Government, who was greatly pleased with Lawry's past history, as well as with his agreeable manners, and his close attention to his business. Through this gentleman, an effort, warmly seconded by Mr. Randall, the bank director, was made to obtain the pardon of John Wilford. It was successful, and the ferryman returned to his home a wiser and a better man.

He was astonished at the operations of his son, and surprised at the prosperity which had attended his family during his absence. The cottage had been enlarged, repaired, painted, and partly refurnished. It was a new home to him; and, profiting by the experience of the past, he resumed his labor as a ferryman, striving to be contented with his lot.

Ethan French does not tire of his pet, the engine of the *Woodville,* though it must be acknowledged that he has a divided heart when Fanny Jane is on board.

Mrs. Wilford, her confidence in her "smart boy" fully justified, and rejoicing in the prosperity which attends him, is still happy and contented in doing a mother's whole duty to her large family of little ones, hoping that all of them will "turn out" as well as her second son.

During the *Woodville's* second business season, she was employed by a party of wealthy gentlemen, for a week, in going round the lake. She had descended the

Richelieu to St. Johns, from which the party ran up to Montreal for a day, returning to the boat in the evening. Though the time for which the boat was engaged was not up till the next evening, some of the gentlemen were very anxious to be in Burlington on the following morning, and insisted that the steamer should immediately proceed up the river on her return. It was a very dark and foggy night, and Lawry declined to start, declaring that he could not run with safety to the boat and passengers.

The party continued to insist upon their point, adding that if he was a competent pilot there could be no difficulty in complying with their wishes. They were gentlemen of wealth and influence, and the little captain did not like to disoblige them. He argued the question with them, and pointed to the motto in the wheelhouse. They laughed at him and his motto. There was to be a "trot" between two celebrated horses, at Burlington, and they were too anxious to witness the race to be entirely reasonable.

Captain Lawry was firm, and the gentlemen were angry and indignant. While they were debating the question in excited tones, another steamer left the wharf, bound up the river. Her departure seemed to spoil the young pilot's argument. The party tried to hail the steamer in the fog, wishing Lawry to put them on board of her; but her people did not hear their demand, or would not stop for them, and the party were highly incensed at what they called the obstinacy of Lawry.

"Haste and waste, gentlemen," replied the little captain. "The river is narrow and crooked, and there is great danger of getting aground if I attempt to run in this fog."

"That other steamer has gone, and if she can run, you can, if you know your business," replied one of the gentlemen.

"I'm very sorry; but I don't think we should gain anything by starting now," added Lawry.

Finding it was useless to insist any longer, the party took supper, and turned in, when their anger had partially subsided. The little captain did not retire that night; he "planked the deck," and watched the weather. It was a seven hours' run to Burlington, and the "trot" was to come off at nine o'clock in the forenoon. He still hoped that he should be able to satisfy his unreasonable party.

At midnight the wind chopped round to the westward, and blew the fog over.

At one o'clock the **Woodville** was going up the river at full speed. At three o'clock she came up with the steamer which had started from St. Johns four hours before, hard and fast aground. She hailed the little **Woodville**, and requested assistance. Lawry took a hawser on board, and gave her a few pulls; but she was too hard on the sand to be started, and he was compelled to abandon her. The commotion caused by these operations awoke some of the gentlemen in the cabin of the **Woodville**, and they came on deck to learn the occasion of it.

"What's the trouble, Captain Lawry?" asked one of them.

"Haste and waste," replied the young pilot sententiously.

"What do you mean?"

"Nothing, only the boat which left St. Johns four hours before us is aground, and can't get off."

"Well, haste and waste does mean something, after all," laughed the speaker.

The gentlemen went to bed again; the **Woodville** continued on her course, and when the party came on deck, at seven in the morning, she was in sight of Burlington. Of course, the excursionists were delighted to be able to attend the "trot." At four o'clock in the afternoon, the steamer which had grounded reached Burlington. Some of Lawry's party came on board in the evening to settle their accounts with the boat. They were gentlemen, and they acknowledged their error, and apologized for the strong language they had used.

"Well, gentlemen, I am very glad you are satisfied," said Lawry, as he put their money in his pocket. "I shall still believe in and follow my motto--HASTE AND WASTE."

The Codes Of Hammurabi And Moses
W. W. Davies

QTY

The discovery of the Hammurabi Code is one of the greatest achievements of archaeology, and is of paramount interest, not only to the student of the Bible, but also to all those interested in ancient history...

Religion   **ISBN: *1-59462-338-4***   **Pages:132**

MSRP $12.95

The Theory of Moral Sentiments
Adam Smith

QTY

This work from 1749. contains original theories of conscience amd moral judgment and it is the foundation for systemof morals.

Philosophy   **ISBN: *1-59462-777-0***   **Pages:536**

MSRP $19.95

Jessica's First Prayer
Hesba Stretton

QTY

In a screened and secluded corner of one of the many railway-bridges which span the streets of London there could be seen a few years ago, from five o'clock every morning until half past eight, a tidily set-out coffee-stall, consisting of a trestle and board, upon which stood two large tin cans, with a small fire of charcoal burning under each so as to keep the coffee boiling during the early hours of the morning when the work-people were thronging into the city on their way to their daily toil...

Pages:84

Childrens   **ISBN: *1-59462-373-2***   *MSRP $9.95*

My Life and Work
Henry Ford

QTY

Henry Ford revolutionized the world with his implementation of mass production for the Model T automobile. Gain valuable business insight into his life and work with his own auto-biography... "We have only started on our development of our country we have not as yet, with all our talk of wonderful progress, done more than scratch the surface. The progress has been wonderful enough but..."

Pages:300

Biographies/   **ISBN: *1-59462-198-5***   *MSRP $21.95*

The Art of Cross-Examination
Francis Wellman

QTY

I presume it is the experience of every author, after his first book is published upon an important subject, to be almost overwhelmed with a wealth of ideas and illustrations which could readily have been included in his book, and which to his own mind, at least, seem to make a second edition inevitable. Such certainly was the case with me; and when the first edition had reached its sixth impression in five months, I rejoiced to learn that it seemed to my publishers that the book had met with a sufficiently favorable reception to justify a second and considerably enlarged edition. ..

Pages:412

Reference   ISBN: *1-59462-647-2*   *MSRP $19.95*

On the Duty of Civil Disobedience
Henry David Thoreau

QTY

Thoreau wrote his famous essay, On the Duty of Civil Disobedience, as a protest against an unjust but popular war and the immoral but popular institution of slave-owning. He did more than write—he declined to pay his taxes, and was hauled off to gaol in consequence. Who can say how much this refusal of his hastened the end of the war and of slavery ?

Law   ISBN: *1-59462-747-9*

Pages:48
MSRP $7.45

Dream Psychology Psychoanalysis for Beginners
Sigmund Freud

QTY

Sigmund Freud, born Sigismund Schlomo Freud (May 6, 1856 - September 23, 1939), was a Jewish-Austrian neurologist and psychiatrist who co-founded the psychoanalytic school of psychology. Freud is best known for his theories of the unconscious mind, especially involving the mechanism of repression; his redefinition of sexual desire as mobile and directed towards a wide variety of objects; and his therapeutic techniques, especially his understanding of transference in the therapeutic relationship and the presumed value of dreams as sources of insight into unconscious desires.

Pages:196

Psychology   ISBN: *1-59462-905-6*   *MSRP $15.45*

The Miracle of Right Thought
Orison Swett Marden

QTY

Believe with all of your heart that you will do what you were made to do. When the mind has once formed the habit of holding cheerful, happy, prosperous pictures, it will not be easy to form the opposite habit. It does not matter how improbable or how far away this realization may see, or how dark the prospects may be, if we visualize them as best we can, as vividly as possible, hold tenaciously to them and vigorously struggle to attain them, they will gradually become actualized, realized in the life. But a desire, a longing without endeavor, a yearning abandoned or held indifferently will vanish without realization.

Pages:360

Self Help   ISBN: *1-59462-644-8*   *MSRP $25.45*

The Rosicrucian Cosmo-Conception Mystic Christianity *by Max Heindel* ISBN: *1-59462-188-8* **$38.95**
The Rosicrucian Cosmo-conception is not dogmatic, neither does it appeal to any other authority than the reason of the student. It is: not controversial, but is: sent forth in the, hope that it may help to clear... New Age/Religion Pages 646

Abandonment To Divine Providence *by Jean-Pierre de Caussade* ISBN: *1-59462-228-0* **$25.95**
"The Rev. Jean Pierre de Caussade was one of the most remarkable spiritual writers of the Society of Jesus in France in the 18th Century. His death took place at Toulouse in 1751. His works have gone through many editions and have been republished... Inspirational/Religion Pages 400

Mental Chemistry *by Charles Haanel* ISBN: *1-59462-192-6* **$23.95**
Mental Chemistry allows the change of material conditions by combining and appropriately utilizing the power of the mind. Much like applied chemistry creates something new and unique out of careful combinations of chemicals the mastery of mental chemistry... New Age Pages 354

The Letters of Robert Browning and Elizabeth Barret Barrett 1845-1846 vol II ISBN: *1-59462-193-4* **$35.95**
by Robert Browning and Elizabeth Barrett Biographies Pages 596

Gleanings In Genesis (volume I) *by Arthur W. Pink* ISBN: *1-59462-130-6* **$27.45**
Appropriately has Genesis been termed "the seed plot of the Bible" for in it we have, in germ form, almost all of the great doctrines which are afterwards fully developed in the books of Scripture which follow... Religion/Inspirational Pages 420

The Master Key *by L. W. de Laurence* ISBN: *1-59462-001-6* **$30.95**
In no branch of human knowledge has there been a more lively increase of the spirit of research during the past few years than in the study of Psychology, Concentration and Mental Discipline. The requests for authentic lessons in Thought Control, Mental Discipline and... New Age/Business Pages 422

The Lesser Key Of Solomon Goetia *by L. W. de Laurence* ISBN: *1-59462-092-X* **$9.95**
This translation of the first book of the "Lernegton" which is now for the first time made accessible to students of Talismanic Magic was done, after careful collation and edition, from numerous Ancient Manuscripts in Hebrew, Latin, and French... New Age/Occult Pages 92

Rubaiyat Of Omar Khayyam *by Edward Fitzgerald* ISBN:*1-59462-332-5* **$13.95**
Edward Fitzgerald, whom the world has already learned, in spite of his own efforts to remain within the shadow of anonymity, to look upon as one of the rarest poets of the century, was born at Bredfield, in Suffolk, on the 31st of March, 1809. He was the third son of John Purcell... Music Pages 172

Ancient Law *by Henry Maine* ISBN: *1-59462-128-4* **$29.95**
The chief object of the following pages is to indicate some of the earliest ideas of mankind, as they are reflected in Ancient Law, and to point out the relation of those ideas to modern thought. Religion/History Pages 452

Far-Away Stories *by William J. Locke* ISBN: *1-59462-129-2* **$19.45**
"Good wine needs no bush, but a collection of mixed vintages does. And this book is just such a collection. Some of the stories I do not want to remain buried for ever in the museum files of dead magazine-numbers an author's not unpardonable vanity..." Fiction Pages 272

Life of David Crockett *by David Crockett* ISBN: *1-59462-250-7* **$27.45**
"Colonel David Crockett was one of the most remarkable men of the times in which he lived. Born in humble life, but gifted with a strong will, an indomitable courage, and unremitting perseverance... Biographies/New Age Pages 424

Lip-Reading *by Edward Nitchie* ISBN: *1-59462-206-X* **$25.95**
Edward B. Nitchie, founder of the New York School for the Hard of Hearing, now the Nitchie School of Lip-Reading, Inc, wrote "LIP-READING Principles and Practice". The development and perfecting of this meritorious work on lip-reading was an undertaking... How-to Pages 400

A Handbook of Suggestive Therapeutics, Applied Hypnotism, Psychic Science ISBN: *1-59462-214-0* **$24.95**
by Henry Munro Health/New Age/Health/Self-help Pages 376

A Doll's House: and Two Other Plays *by Henrik Ibsen* ISBN: *1-59462-112-8* **$19.95**
Henrik Ibsen created this classic when in revolutionary 1848 Rome. Introducing some striking concepts in playwriting for the realist genre, this play has been studied the world over. Fiction/Classics/Plays 308

The Light of Asia *by sir Edwin Arnold* ISBN: *1-59462-204-3* **$13.95**
In this poetic masterpiece, Edwin Arnold describes the life and teachings of Buddha. The man who was to become known as Buddha to the world was born as Prince Gautama of India but he rejected the worldly riches and abandoned the reigns of power when... Religion/History/Biographies Pages 170

The Complete Works of Guy de Maupassant *by Guy de Maupassant* ISBN: *1-59462-157-8* **$16.95**
"For days and days, nights and nights, I had dreamed of that first kiss which was to consecrate our engagement, and I knew not on what spot I should put my lips..." Fiction/Classics Pages 240

The Art of Cross-Examination *by Francis L. Wellman* ISBN: *1-59462-309-0* **$26.95**
Written by a renowned trial lawyer, Wellman imparts his experience and uses case studies to explain how to use psychology to extract desired information through questioning. How-to/Science/Reference Pages 408

Answered or Unanswered? *by Louisa Vaughan* ISBN: *1-59462-248-5* **$10.95**
Miracles of Faith in China Religion Pages 112

The Edinburgh Lectures on Mental Science (1909) *by Thomas* ISBN: *1-59462-008-3* **$11.95**
This book contains the substance of a course of lectures recently given by the writer in the Queen Street Hall, Edinburgh. Its purpose is to indicate the Natural Principles governing the relation between Mental Action and Material Conditions... New Age/Psychology Pages 148

Ayesha *by H. Rider Haggard* ISBN: *1-59462-301-5* **$24.95**
Verily and indeed it is the unexpected that happens! Probably if there was one person upon the earth from whom the Editor of this, and of a certain previous history, did not expect to hear again... Classics Pages 380

Ayala's Angel *by Anthony Trollope* ISBN: *1-59462-352-X* **$29.95**
The two girls were both pretty, but Lucy who was twenty-one who supposed to be simple and comparatively unattractive, whereas Ayala was credited, as her Bombwhat romantic name might show, with poetic charm and a taste for romance. Ayala when her father died was nineteen... Fiction Pages 484

The American Commonwealth *by James Bryce* ISBN: *1-59462-286-8* **$34.45**
An interpretation of American democratic political theory. It examines political mechanics and society from the perspective of Scotsman James Bryce Politics Pages 572

Stories of the Pilgrims *by Margaret P. Pumphrey* ISBN: *1-59462-116-0* **$17.95**
This book explores pilgrims religious oppression in England as well as their escape to Holland and eventual crossing to America on the Mayflower, and their early days in New England... History Pages 268

www.bookjungle.com *email: sales@bookjungle.com fax: 630-214-0564 mail: Book Jungle PO Box 2226 Champaign, IL 61825*

QTY

The Fasting Cure by *Sinclair Upton*   ISBN: *1-59462-222-1*   **$13.95** ☐
In the Cosmopolitan Magazine for May, 1910, and in the Contemporary Review (London) for April, 1910, I published an article dealing with my experiences in fasting. I have written a great many magazine articles, but never one which attracted so much attention... New Age/Self Help/Health Pages 164

Hebrew Astrology by *Sepharial*   ISBN: *1-59462-308-2*   **$13.45** ☐
In these days of advanced thinking it is a matter of common observation that we have left many of the old landmarks behind and that we are now pressing forward to greater heights and to a wider horizon than that which represented the mind-content of our progenitors... Astrology Pages 144

Thought Vibration or The Law of Attraction in the Thought World   ISBN: *1-59462-127-6*   **$12.95** ☐
by *William Walker Atkinson*   Psychology/Religion Pages 144

Optimism by *Helen Keller*   ISBN: *1-59462-108-X*   **$15.95** ☐
Helen Keller was blind, deaf, and mute since 19 months old, yet famously learned how to overcome these handicaps, communicate with the world, and spread her lectures promoting optimism. An inspiring read for everyone... Biographies/Inspirational Pages 84

Sara Crewe by *Frances Burnett*   ISBN: *1-59462-360-0*   **$9.45** ☐
In the first place, Miss Minchin lived in London. Her home was a large, dull, tall one, in a large, dull square, where all the houses were alike, and all the sparrows were alike, and where all the door-knockers made the same heavy sound... Childrens/Classic Pages 88

The Autobiography of Benjamin Franklin by *Benjamin Franklin*   ISBN: *1-59462-135-7*   **$24.95** ☐
The Autobiography of Benjamin Franklin has probably been more extensively read than any other American historical work, and no other book of its kind has had such ups and downs of fortune. Franklin lived for many years in England, where he was agent... Biographies/History Pages 332

Name	
Email	
Telephone	
Address	
City, State ZIP	

☐ **Credit Card**   ☐ **Check / Money Order**

Credit Card Number	
Expiration Date	
Signature	

Please Mail to: Book Jungle
PO Box 2226
Champaign, IL 61825
or Fax to: 630-214-0564

ORDERING INFORMATION

web: *www.bookjungle.com*
email: *sales@bookjungle.com*
fax: *630-214-0564*
mail: *Book Jungle PO Box 2226 Champaign, IL 61825*
or PayPal *to sales@bookjungle.com*

Please contact us for bulk discounts

DIRECT-ORDER TERMS

**20% Discount if You Order
Two or More Books**
Free Domestic Shipping!
Accepted: Master Card, Visa,
Discover, American Express

www.ingramcontent.com/pod-product-compliance
Lightning Source LLC
Chambersburg PA
CBHW080734250626
47170CB00010B/2829